Assassin's Crossfire

Books by Stephen L. Thompson

The Crossfire Series

Colorado Crossfire
International Crossfire
Israeli Crossfire
Believer's Crossfire
Spirit Crossfire
Faith Crossfire
Chinese Crossfire
Texas Crossfire
Dark Crossfire
Island Crossfire
Jagged Crossfire
Violent Crossfire
Russian Crossfire
Nuclear Crossfire
End Times Crossfire
Revelation Crossfire
Gates of Hell Crossfire
Assassin's Crossfire
Global Crossfire
Far East Crossfire

The SFO Series

Station Force One - Onset

Assassin's Crossfire

"One Evil Thing After Another"

Stephen L. Thompson

Assassin's Crossfire

The Crossfire Team has destroyed part of Satan's demonic domain as Yahveh commanded them to do. Now Satan has goaded the RHONE to attack the Team with their entire professional and contract assassins in an attempt to eliminate God's warriors. The resultant actions cause the Team to step up their efforts to eliminate the RHONE completely

-   Stephen L. Thompson

Assassin's Crossfire

Published by
Stephen L. Thompson
Facebook.com/CrossfireNovelSeries

Unless otherwise noted, Scripture quotations are taken from the HOLY BIBLE, NEW INTERNATIONAL VERSION®. Copyright© 1973, 1978, 1984 by International Bible Society. Used by permission of Zondervan Publishing House. All rights reserved.

ISBN - 978-1-943879-23-6

Published in the United States of America

Foreword

To my Christian readers –
The Crossfire continuing series of action-adventure novels include depictions of violence which are unusual in Christian literature. It would be nice if there were no conflict or violence in our world. But we live in a time when evil is increasing instead of diminishing, when some men seem to be controlled by selfishness, madness, or evil forces. When the enemies of decent mankind are bent on subjugation of other men and women, righteous men and women must stand against evil. The yoke of oppression is not lifted by prayer alone. God is our shepherd and we are his sheep. As long as there are wolves about, God will use some of us as sheep dogs to defend the rest of us. These stories are about people like that and the forces they fight against. The stories describe violence because it occurs in the real world and it is active in the lives of all people whether they recognize it or not.

To my non-Christian readers –
The Crossfire series include depictions of spiritual warfare and spiritual activity with which the non-Christian reader may not be familiar. These stories describe the realms and activities of both God and Satan because they're real and active in the lives of all people whether they recognize it or not.

Steve Thompson

CHAPTER ONE

At a signal from the large, muscular man on her right side, the woman gracefully stood up between the two men and looked at the smaller man behind the fake-wood desk.

Knowing she looked like a small book between two big bookends she gathered her strength. Sarah turned and smiled at the big man on her right and started to lean back at the waist. As the man leaned toward her to stop her from getting away Sarah suddenly bent forward using the full body torque from her waist upward she snapped her forehead forward into the bigger man's face. His nose was crushed flat and he stumbled backward covering the damage to his face with his hands.

Sarah continued to move as she spun around to her left on the ball of her left foot and raised her right leg, pulling her right foot all the way up to her buttocks. She snapped her right foot forward with all the power she could muster. Sarah timed it out and quickly bent backward at the waist again; both to avoid the clutching arms of big man number two and to add to the power of her kick. By throwing her shoulders and head back against the leg muscle extension, she was able to add full body torque to the kick. Her foot sank into the second man's stomach so hard it kicked his feet out from below him.

As Sarah was bringing her right foot back to the ground, she saw the suddenly frightened man at the desk pulling a pistol from his right top hand drawer. Since her right leg was still in the air and her skirt had slid up to reveal her holster, her right hand found her automatic on her thigh and fired while it was still in its holster. She didn't have time to draw and fire. Fortunately, she had practiced this exact tactic hundreds of times and her aim was true. The bullet smashed through the man's right shoulder. The pistol flew from his hand as the bullet slammed into the wall behind him.

Sarah continued to pull her handgun out of the holster. She then smashed the barrel down onto the head of the man she had just kicked, as he was still falling to the floor. She then aimed the pistol at the man with the bloody nose.

Fortunately, for him, he was still trying to stop the tears in his eyes long enough to see his attacker. Sarah stepped forward on the ball of her left foot and kicked the first muscle man between the legs hard enough to lift him off the floor. This additional abuse was enough to make him fall forward clutching his groin with hands still bloody from his nose. Sarah then brought the handgun down on the back of his head with sufficient force to make him forget his pains in both ends of his body and drop unconscious to the floor. Sarah then aimed the pistol at the man at the desk who was now doing nothing but screaming loudly and staring at his wounded shoulder.

Sarah stepped over the body of the second guard and walked around the desk. She pulled a syringe out of her coat pocket, pulled the cover off of the needle, cleared any air from the needle and jabbed the needle into desk man's neck. He stopped screaming in pain, looked at her with big, wide-open eyes and then fell back in his chair, unconscious.

Sarah heard the rush of footsteps toward the closed office door. She lightly ran to the wall next to the door. When the receptionist opened the door and stepped into the room her hand flew to her mouth and Sarah could see her filling her lungs to let out a loud scream. Sarah tapped the woman on the arm. She turned wide-eyed to see who it was. Sarah drove a fist into the panicked woman's stomach and the air flew out of her mouth with a rush and she fell to her knees trying to get her breath.

Sarah pulled out a second syringe and sent the gasping woman off to dreamland. As her head slowly joined her knees on the floor she fell to her left side. Sarah looked out the door and saw nothing and no one. She shut the door and leaned against the wall with a smile. That was an excellent workout. Her mind recalled her immediate past to make sense of the mayhem she had just caused.

-------------------------*****-------------------------

It was a nice day in the business suburb as Sarah Connelly casually walked up to the nondescript office building front in Tel Aviv, Israel, and asked the receptionist if she could see Mr. Trevant. The receptionist made a phone call and then ushered the visitor into a plush office suite.

A young man stepped out from behind his desk and came forward and shook the young woman's hand. "How may I help you?"

She smiled at him and asked if he was acquainted with a Mr. Harbinger. Mr. Trevant stepped back and stared at her. "May I ask what business you have with Mr. Harbinger?"

She glanced down for a second and then looked him in the eye and calmly said, "I represent the Crossfire Team and we want to discuss some mutual business with him."

Mr. Trevant showed her to a seat in front of his desk and he went behind the desk and sat down. As he looked at the woman he used his right foot to press a button on the lower inside of the panel to the right of his feet. "I will see if I can contact Mr. Harbinger for you."

Two men quietly entered the office behind Sarah and silently moved up behind her. Both of these men were young and solidly built. Their hard facial expressions indicated that they were all business. Sarah Connelly ignored them completely and kept her eyes on Mr. Trevant. She quietly said, "This day I call the heavens and the earth as witnesses against you that I have set before you; life and death, blessings and curses. Now choose life, so that you may live."

Mr. Trevant laughed at the young woman. "I have all the cards on my side of this game, young woman. I will give you the same offer. What is your name?"

She smiled at him. "My name is unimportant as I am only a messenger, offering you a choice. Make your decision carefully as it could be the last one you make before you meet the God that made that statement in Deuteronomy 30:19."

Mr. Trevant told the two men to take her to their party room and teach her to be more respectful.

-----------------------*****-----------------------

Sarah's memories and her present came together and she spoke into the air. "I have two for speaking engagements and two for tying up loose ends. Please do this quickly, because they are not happy here."

Three minutes later, her husband, Mark Connelly, along with David Zahavy and Megan Cole walked into the room with two body bags and four sets of riot cuffs. Mark looked like an on-duty U.S. Marine, all business. He cuffed the receptionist and both of the beefy security types and then laid the other set of riot cuffs on the desk in front of Mr. Trevant.

David Zahavy looked like a professional Israeli business man that dressed very fashionably. He had pulled the jacket and shirt off of the man at the desk and was checking the through-and-through wound to the man's shoulder. Nothing seemed to be broken and the wounds both in and out weren't bleeding, too much, so no major arteries were cut. He poured sulfa powder into both wounds and bandaged them securely. The he used the riot cuffs and bound the sleeping man's hands.

Megan Cole looked like a tri-athlete and possibly a weight lifter. She stood guard over the operations with her handgun in her hand. Looking at her, one could see that she knew how to use it.

Mark had pried the bullet out of the wall from the shot Sarah had used to wound the man and placed it into a small plastic bag and took off his plastic gloves. He helped David get the man into one of the body bags. Sarah and Megan got the receptionist into the other body bag. The four people then picked up the two bags and carried them out of the building. They placed the bags into the back of an idling van. David climbed into the back with the sedated couple. Mark closed the back doors. He got into the driver's seat of the van with Sarah beside him and Megan riding shotgun.

Mark carefully pulled out into afternoon traffic and quickly became lost in the traffic of Tel Aviv.

CHAPTER TWO

After the Mossad interrogators were finished with both the underboss and the receptionist they were re-sedated and taken to a motel room where they were left sleeping off the drugs. Neither one of them had seen anything during their trip.

The information the interrogators had gotten was considerable and valuable. At least it was to the Crossfire Team. It gave them all the pieces to the assassin puzzle they were attempting to overcome. They now had photos of all the RHONE SS assassins and of all the contract assassins in the Nation of Israel. The RHONE was the military and execution arm of the Anti-Christ, Marco Marino.

That evening, they worked the "Bait" operation for the third night in a row. Jack Malone had almost cancelled the operation because the attackers were becoming more vicious and deadly. In cooperation with the Mayor and the Police Chief of Tel Aviv, the area had been subtly blocked off to protect innocent civilians.

Sixteen RHONE snipers working in unison attacked at one time. Acting as an Anti-Sniper, Jack took a shot and eliminated one of the RHONE snipers and rolled onto his back and traded shots with another four assassins behind them that had targeted both him and Mark. He took another one down and rolled back to help the "bait" on the streets below to survive their attacks.

Mark took a round in his armored back and another on his helmet that ricocheted. He rolled over and fired back at the shooters and hit both of them. He watched as his backup, Phil Austin took out another one of the rooftop attackers. In his ear he heard Charlie Wu's warning and Mark started praying. It was the first time his silver armor and the sword of God's Word appeared while he was laying on his back. He scrambled to his feet and his armor deflected three more rounds from the other assassins as a demon appeared and charged at Jack who was still trading fire with two RHONE assassins on other rooftops.

Mark ran to his left and intercepted the creature and attacked it. The demon turned to fight the silver armored warrior only to see its black blade shattered by the bright sword of Mark's that was streaming with the essence of Yahveh. Mark rammed his blade up through the jaw and head of the demon twisted it to hasten the demon's end and turned to attack the assassins on their roof. He took another shot from an assassin on a different roof that spun him around but didn't penetrate the armor. He advanced on the assassins as one of them was killed by Phil. The other one wanted to run but as he turned, two more demons appeared and the larger demon ran the assassin through with its sword for retreating and so that it could get directly at Mark.

Four rounds from Phil Austin punched big holes in the second demon that was obviously in our dimension without God's permission.

The demon attacking Mark was smaller than most demons and almost human in size and appearance. Its skin was a deep black and its eyes were red. It squared up with Mark as two of Phil's rounds hit it and did not affect it. It didn't act like a normal demon which would race into battle. It started stalking Mark on the roof top. Mark cut off its advance and swung a direct strike with his sword from right to left. The demon blocked the swing with its black sword and Mark's sword was deflected.

Even though he was surprised that the sword of the Word with Yahveh's glory streaming off of the blade didn't break the demon's sword, Mark stepped back and brought his sword up to a defensive position from which he deflected the thin black blade of the demon.

For the first time since he was anointed with his sword and armor Mark realized he was in for an actual sword fight. He stepped back and prayed for Yahveh's blessing on his ability to compete with this agent of darkness.

The demon started slashing and thrusting at Mark who deflected the blade and looked for an opening. The demon did a thrust that Mark deflected to his right. A memory appeared in Mark's mind from his training with Hugo on sword fighting. This thrust would cause the demon to whirl around to its left and do a cross body slash after it returned to a face-to-face position with Mark.

As the demon released the thrust and started to turn, Mark lunged at the demon and ran it through with his sword. Mark then twisted his sword to increase the internal damage to the demon. The demon screamed and dropped its sword as it fell forward, away from Mark, to the roof top and dissipated into a foul red smoke.

Mark stopped praying and ran back to his rifle as his armor disappeared. He took his spot on the roof's edge and started to look for more shooters.

The original four snipers' intent on killing the two Team members on the street had held back so that the six Crossfire Team counter snipers couldn't find them until the actual moment of the attack. Each one suddenly stepped to the doorway or window and aimed and fired at the two team members on the street.

Charlie Wu had spotted one of the snipers just before they moved and warned the two team members on the street. Ethan and Su Li each threw themselves apart from each other with Ethan going to the pavement next to a parked car and Su Li went into a niche in a wall. They both made themselves as small a target as possible. Bullets struck around them, hit the car and the wall and ricocheted all over the place.

The counter snipers on the team responded immediately and took out three of the shooters in their original volley. The fourth one had jumped back into the apartment or room she and a backup were in, just to avoid that fire. What that woman didn't expect was the follow-up 40mm grenade's fleshettes that were fired as an insurance round into the room. She and her backup died instantly.

With all the team snipers focused on the scene below them they were vulnerable to attack themselves by both assassins and demons. They had experienced this type of double layer assassin attack on their first two attempts. Now, each shooter had another Core Team member or SOG member as backup and they had Charlie watching for demonic signs to warn them. Mark's mind had a combat flash of memory concerning this setup.

-----------------------******-----------------------

Jack and Mark had been laying twenty feet apart on the roof of a ten story business building overlooking two streets and the intersection between them. Ethan and Su Li were on the street below Mark, headed east toward the intersection where they were to turn right under Jack's sights. There weren't any citizens or shoppers on the streets tonight compared to the previous two nights.

Mark and Sarah had just finished the dangerous role of being "bait" last night while the rest of the team tried to eliminate the RHONE's assassins and the contract assassins the RHONE was sponsoring. The "bait" had to be on the highest level alert for assassins. They could be on the street, in widows of buildings, in cars and trucks, in alleys and simply sitting in a café or coming out of a store.

All six of the anti-sniper snipers and two backup resource personnel were orbiting around the "bait" attempting to find the snipers before they acted and tried to take out the "bait" or the counter snipers. They had resorted to having a backup warrior for all of the team members supporting the "bait".

-----------------------******-----------------------

Mark's memory snapped back into reality as he spotted another assassin with a rifle. Mark snap aimed and fired his rifle. The .50 caliber round drilled the assassin through the throat which almost tore the man's head off. The already dead assassin fell back out of the window into the room he had been in and dropped his rifle to the street below.

Ethan snuck up to Su Li's position in the notch in the wall and whispered, "I think we need to move before they can move in on us."

Su Li leaned back against the wall for cover and carefully stood up and looked around. "Too late, I think they are already here." She took out her Sig-Sauer .40 caliber handgun and crouched down again as she targeted one of the many attackers moving toward her and Ethan. She spoke into the bone conduction combat net microphone at her ear, "All counter snipers; we have multiple targets on the ground moving in on us."

She was fired on and returned the fire as more and more people drew handguns or displayed rifles they had hidden under their coats. Suddenly, the incoming fire against the assassins was multiplied terrifically. Not only were the counter snipers weighing in but ten to twenty people on the street were behind vehicles or some sort of shelter and were shooting at the assassins and taking them down. Su Li and Ethan added their pistols to the volume of fire against the assassins. The battle was lop-sided against the assassins and over quickly.

While the counter snipers continued to watch for more shooters, Ethan and Su Li moved out to check the assassins for any sign of life.

None of the eleven assassins had survived the one sided slaughter. Su Li looked at one of the "public" that had contributed to their survival and realized he had a badge that identified him as a member of the Mossad, probably a Kidon assassin himself. She said, "Thanks."

He looked at her and smiled, "Glad to be of help. You people need to realize that others can help too." He waved his hand to encompass all the people on the street. "Everyone here is off-duty Mossad or IDF risking their lives to help you and your teammates eliminate these killers."

Su Li nodded her head, "Speaking for the team I thank you and clearly understand the danger. I believe that the assassins changed the game with these mass attacks tonight. I'm sure that Jack Malone will be very appreciative of your efforts concerning our attackers."

The Mossad officer nodded his head, "I am glad and I will pass that onto my superiors. I know our groups also appreciate the fact that your team got permission from the city leaders, Tel Aviv Police, and the Israeli military to protect the city and its citizens."

Jack walked up to the little group and introduced himself to the officer. "I heard a little bit of your last conversation and want to add my appreciation to your efforts. I sought out and secured permission from the city, the police, and General Levy of the IDF, before we started this operation. They understood the danger of this type of combat in the city but they also endorsed the need to draw out the assassins. Well, tonight proved that using our members as bait is no longer an option. The RHONE is not concerned about collateral damage like we are. I assume that is why you and your forces are out here and I really appreciate your assistance and bravery for exposing yourselves to a danger that really wasn't yours."

The Mossad officer shook Jack's hand and said, "We, thank you for not being the "Cowboys" some of us thought you were."

Jack nodded, and shook hands with the officer. Then he used his combat microphone to have all Team forces return to the Sea Base.

After cleaning up and resting, the Core Team met in the War Room and discussed the situation. Jack showed the videos of all the action that Charlie had gathered for Ethan since Ethan had to play "bait" this evening.

Jack shook his head, "It is obvious that the RHONE takes its marching orders from the demonic. The demonic tried to overwhelm us, which didn't work out too well for them. I understand that the demonic kingdom over Israel is down to eighty percent of what it was before I closed their rifts with nuclear weapons. Incidentally, that is why the RHONE assassins are after us in the first place. But, this "overwhelming" didn't work for the assassins either. Now we have to come up with something serious enough to make the RHONE want to leave us alone.

CHAPTER THREE

In a hotel room in South Tel Aviv, four miles from the Portal; nine of the RHONE assassins were meeting. The general atmosphere was anger and frustration.

Arthur Spenser had been killing people for the RHONE for over ten years and had never suffered a defeat such as the assassins had this evening. His anger was; one-part personal failure, one-part group failure, and one-part fear of the RHONE leadership. He was quite sure that the leadership in Bern already knew of their third defeat in three nights. Adding to his frustration was the fact that he was the one that planned all three of the assaults. Now each one had been a defeat that had cost them over twenty-three of their people and they had not even wounded one of their targets.

Milo Zakius had sat through Spenser's litany of regrets and forebodings as long as he could. He stood up and got everyone's attention. "All right Spenser, you've identified all our shortcomings and convinced me that we have killed over twelve percent of the entire assassin's group of the RHONE" He was even angrier than Spenser. "WHAT are YOU going to do about completing our mission? If you don't know then let someone else do the planning!"

Spenser stared at the Sicilian with contempt. He thought to himself, "How can this scum talk to me this way? I should kill him right now. But, we're short of people and it would not make my masters happy. "Shut up Zakius! You are the least of us here and not qualified to judge my efforts. Sit down!"

Zakius was also considering murder when he felt a fire in his head that was so hot it was burning his brain. He tried to scream but only blood came out of his mouth and nose. He flailed around and then fell to the floor. His sightless eyes had a look of horror of what he had seen just before he died.

Even Spenser was frightened by the execution which, by extension, could happen to everyone here including himself. It was an object lesson by the ruling group. Don't buck the system or you will die horribly.

Spenser had two of the men drag the corpse into the next room. They would deal with it later. No one was objecting to Spenser's commands now.

Spenser thought about their main problem. They could not get to the Crossfire Team in whatever lair they lived in and they had no idea of when or where they would get a target at this point.

Suddenly Spenser had a thought that wasn't his. He knew it wasn't his because it contained information he had never known before, details never considered, and it felt slimy and somewhat evil.

He looked at the other seven men and nodded his head. "All right, listen up. We are going to have a shot at the leader of this accursed team in the next several weeks. Jack Malone is going to be hunted by the Tel Aviv Police and the Mossad and it will be our job to make sure he is never found alive. When the time is right and this event is about to happen, I will contact each of you. Right now I am going to give each of you a list of three names. These are not our co-workers; they are contract assassins. I want each of you to bring them in over the next two weeks and whip them into shape to work with us."

He pointed at one of the men that had moved the body into the next room. "Go in the other room and take a couple of pictures of Zakius. Get a close-up of his face. Use that to "encourage" the new people to toe the line, or else."

Spenser then added, "I want a net that will catch Malone and dispose of him. You are dismissed."

As the other seven men left the hotel room for wherever they were staying, Spenser called down to the special bell hop that worked at his hotel and arranged to dispose of the body in the next room. His phone chimed to tell him he now had a copy of the pictures of the dead man to use.

Spenser arranged to have his belongings moved to a new room while the bell hop disposed of Zakius' body. He wanted to feel better about things but knew from the message he had received that the next operation had better work or he wouldn't get another chance.

CHAPTER FOUR

Charlie Wu came into the War Room and sat down in his position at the new circular conference table. There were twenty positions in groups of two with an empty position between those groups and the next set of two positions. This was a major change from what Laura had expected after telling facilities that the people on the end of the original table were not able to see the big screen. Originally they were going to put in cubes stacked on top of each other all facing the big screen.

Now, the table was completely circular so that everyone could see the others at the table face to face. The table was only twenty-five feet in diameter, fifteen feet less than before. Facilities had resolved the problem of the big screen. Each pair of positions saw the big screen above and behind the positions at the other side of the table. The Engineers at Facilities had replaced the single big screen with a virtual copy that was bright and clear directly across the table from each group. If someone used a laser pointer it showed on all of the virtual screens at the correct location. Plus, every position had full communications and access to all of the COMM/SEC services and video feeds.

Charlie was a young expatriate Chinese Internal Security Agent that had found Yahshua and escaped to the West with his wife, Linda, who had also been an agent. They had to leave when their Christian religion was discovered. From his calm demeanor and unlined face that didn't display his emotions he was unreadable. His quick mind and vast experience had been an immeasurable asset to the Crossfire Team since the beginnings of the team.

He stood about five foot nine inches tall and had a full head of black hair. His wiry frame was much stronger than it looked and his capabilities in Martial Arts and weapons were outstanding. He did have a good sense of humor and liked to mess with people's minds. He had designed and set up the COMM/SEC department and ran it for the first eighteen months. He and his wife had just turned the operation over to Ethan Reaper as they became a more active part of the combat team.

Charlie looked at Mark Connelly, "Mark, I think I know how we can send a message to the RHONE to back off. We could simply kill them. But, when I prayed about it I didn't get a leading that we should do that, not yet. Yahveh hasn't released us to just cut off the head of the snake until we have graphically shown them that they are vulnerable and then they can choose to ignore the warning. Sort of like the submarine and the choice they made."

Laura spoke up, "I think Charlie is right. We need to stop these assassin attacks but it is got to be done God's way. He would warn them first. If they don't stop the attacks, then we will be released to terminate them."

Mark looked at the Asian, "I agree, what have you determined would give them a real reason to be afraid and have to make that choice?"

Charlie smiled and began to explain his idea.

Three weeks later, Mark Connelly and Charlie Wu sat quietly in the large panel van watching the new headquarters of the Revived Highest Order Nazi Empire (RHONE) on a large video screen on the outskirts of Bern, Switzerland.

This modern building and its grounds were carefully laid out to provide defensive security and to make a definite statement that this is where the power was located.

The RHONE was a 200,000-member private army that was under the total control of Marco Marino, the leader of the New World Order. The building itself was located just two miles SSW of Bern. Access to the site was highly restricted and over a hundred heavily armed RHONE soldiers were on high alert.

The new dedication ceremony was about to begin and the top officials of the RHONE were outside, taking their seats on the seven tier grandstand to officiate the ceremony. Charlie hit one button on the keyboard in front of him and a second large video screen showed a selected group of people on the grandstand and in the windows of the building. Charlie pushed another button and used a mouse to select the desired targets.

The new leader of the RHONE walked to the microphone on the stage to announce the dedication. He smiled at everyone and started to speak.

Charlie pushed the second button and watched the output of the camera on the mini-drone dropping straight down toward the ceremony from twelve thousand feet over the mountain city. The small drone leveled off ten feet above the ground and the eight computer-controlled barrels of the twenty-two caliber Gatling gun fired twenty-four times in less than three seconds. Seven people in the widows of the building and sixteen on the platform or on the grandstand were splattered by red paint before anyone knew what was happening. The leader and his cabinet and the head of international net work were among those targeted. The other two hundred people were essentially unhurt. The drone accelerated quickly and immediately flew past the building and out over the river where it ignited a thermal charge that melted the entire drone to ashes before they floated down to land in the river.

Pandemonium reigned at the ceremony site as everyone tried to get off the platform and the grandstand and into the building for safety. Mark turned up the audio to go with the video on one screen to catch the dialog after the leader got into the building.

They listened to his angry screaming and yelling and let the computers back at the Sea Base outside of Israel translate the conversations. He smiled as he listened to the recriminations that the leader laid on the security troop leaders and his own defensive guard. After they listened long enough Charlie broke the connection and sent the entire audio/video package to the Sea Base. Shutting down the electronics in the van he reloaded them and the stools they had been sitting on into the crates they had come from.

Mark then drove the van to the Bern-Belp Airport and had the crates loaded on a flight to Berlin, Germany where they met Su Li, the team pilot and they headed back to Israel.

Mark and Su Li discussed the attack during the two-hour flight back to the Sea Base.

She smiled at Mark. "Did you achieve the desired result you wanted?"

Mark nodded his head. "I think the message got through loud and clear. Now they will either shut down the assault on us or intensify it. They have been warned that if they don't shut it down then they will suffer a worse visit."

After landing at the undersea base Su Li had the crates of equipment moved into the receiving bay and Mark went up to the War Room.

Jack and Laura met him there and they all listened to the solid-state memory of the conversations.

RHONE Leader: "You IDIOTS! How could you allow us to be attacked like that?"

Security Chief: "We never saw the drone until it fired its paintballs. No one was killed and we are attempting to track the electronics that controlled the drone as we speak."

RHONE Leader: "I could have been killed! What type of idiot goes to such expense to shoot us with paintballs?

Security Chief: "We think it was a warning. The warning was to let us know that we are vulnerable and need to stop whatever we are doing or suffer the consequences. Those paintballs could have been bullets and someone else would be having this discussion."

RHONE Leader: "This is intolerable! Find who did this and punish them. Do it quickly or I will transfer their punishment to you! Do you understand me?"

Security Chief: "Yes Sir. Immediately Sir. Excuse me Sir, what is that on your jacket?"

RHONE Leader: "I just don't ...What? What is this?"

Security Chief: "It looks like a bug." Crunch, ting, snap. Then silence.

Mark smiled, "They found the bug the drone placed on the leader. I was sure that they'd find it before then.

Jack shook his head. "It doesn't sound too good for them. I think we will have to make it the real thing next time."

Mark shook his head. "They are either more intensely stupid than I can imagine or they are more driven by their demons than they are by human sense."

Charlie smiled, "No problem, I have their photos and biometrics and we can tag them one at a time if we have to."

CHAPTER FIVE

After he completed teaching a combat class, Mark called Jack and asked to meet at the dining room next to the living room ten minutes from then.

Mark showed up ten minutes later to find Jack sitting there with a cup of coffee. Mark saw that Jack had gotten a cup for him so he sat down across the table. Mark looked like a weight lifter and a marathon runner. He stood six foot, two inches tall and weighed a little over two hundred pounds with eight percent body fat. A solid, good looking young man he had a firm jaw and a solid face that reflected his honesty and drive.

Jack was two inches taller than Mark and weighed fourteen pounds less. Jack's blonde hair contrasted with the black hair of Mark. Jack was less bulked out than Mark but was very strong and equally determined. Since they had met each other almost four years ago they had become best friends and warriors with a shared history of combat and survival.

Jack looked at the muted distress on Mark's face and asked, "What's the problem, buddy?"

Mark set his coffee down on the table. "Three weeks ago when we got jumped on the rooftop I fought with two demons. The first one was a normal slam dunk, straight to the pit. The second one looked almost like a demonized human rather than large, ugly, and brutish. When I struck his blade it deflected my blade. I was praying strength and with passion to the Father but I couldn't break his blade. I actually had a sword fight with this demon."

"Your training kept me from being skewered by his blade but it was some of Hugo's training that let me catch the demon in a sword fighting mistake. I had deflected his blade to my right side and a technique that Hugo showed us let me know that the demon was going to spin around to his left and cross cut me. As he released and started to spin I was able to drive my blade into his right side and kill him. My problem is this. Why couldn't I break his blade? Why did we end up on equal footing and had to actually have a sword fight? I believed that the glory of Yahveh on our swords would overpower the enemy and give us an advantage. What changed?"

Jack shook his head, "I don't know, let's pray about it."

Suddenly the Archangel, Raquel, appeared next to Jack with his own cup of coffee. Jack turned his head and laughed. "It's the answer man."

Raquel smiled at Jack and shook his head. "Actually I am here to assist you in an oncoming problem but I will answer anything I can for you."

Mark retold his story and stared at Raquel.

Raquel looked far away for a short time and then nodded his head. "I have been concerned about this for quite a while. It is actually happening much later than I expected." He looked at Mark and his golden eyes seemed to look right through Mark. He turned to Jack to include him. "The enemy is not dumb. They are not creative but they are sly and conniving. As I said, I'm amazed that they have not started to think through their efforts to eliminate you, as a team. They made several attempts including the time at the hotel in Tel Aviv when your sword would destroy all but one demon. Your combat last night is a new approach they have determined to limit your team's effectiveness."

Jack asked, "What do you mean a new approach?"

Raquel sighed, a very human expression of frustration. The demon you faced last night is actually a higher level demon than the ones you normally face. While it isn't an Archangel level it is higher than the normal demon. That is why you weren't able to simply cut it in half like you are used to doing. As Hugo explained, that demon's unrighteousness was higher than the normal demon's unrighteousness. In the spiritual world righteousness is power but, so is unrighteousness."

Jack asked, "You mean like the unrighteousness of Belial where our swords could not hurt him?"

Raquel nodded, "But, many levels below him. This demon, which I call a middle weight demon, isn't able to overcome your armor or sword completely like Quixapac, only partially. It actually puts you and them on the same level and you have no overwhelming advantage. It is like it was another human being. You can kill them or they can kill you and it is the best warrior that wins. This is the evolution of their efforts against the Crossfire Team. I believe you and your team will be running into more of these middle weight demons in the future. I will bring this to the Most High's attention and see what He wants to do. This is above of my pay grade as you humans would say."

Raquel turned to Jack completely. "There is a very hard period coming for you very soon. Carol won't see it coming and this is the only warning I can give you. Keep your faith and pray that the Father and the Son will be with you during this time. I will be watching over you but this event and the results of it must happen. Do not fear and stay true to your calling."

Raquel faded out of sight.

Jack looked at Mark with concern. "What do you think that means?"

Mark shook his head and sighed. "I don't know but it looks like we need to make some arrangements right now." Mark used his battle communications microphone he was still wearing after the combat class and asked for a quick Core Team meeting at the lunch room.

After Laura, Sarah, David, Alexis, Su Li, Ethan, Megan Cole, Mike White, and Charlie along with Linda arrived and sat down, Jack told them the warning he had just gotten from Raquel. "I don't have any reason to worry but let's face it. The devil is coming against us with all the weapons he has so let's do some emergency planning just in case."

He looked at Laura, "In the event I am sidelined somehow, I want Mark to assume my position as the leader of the Crossfire Team. I also want Laura, and Sarah to function as backup leaders if anything happens to Mark. Does everybody understand?"

After the others agreed Jack continued, "Ethan, I want you to create an unknown and untraceable communications link between Mark and I, Laura and I, and Sarah and all of the four of us. I need that, sort of like a burn phone, by the time I get back from the Mossad Director's office."

Ethan nodded and got up and left for COMM/SEC. Jack looked at the others. "I want Charlie and Linda to oversee Ethan and the COMM/SEC group in my absence or that of any number of us who are unable to function as control. David, I want you and Alexis to unilaterally investigate and determine our absences and or our inability to function as the leaders of the Team."

"Su Li, I want you and Megan to function as the eyes and ears of the Team in our absences or as needed. That will include rescues and protection depending on the circumstances."

Now, I don't expect any of us to have any problems but we twelve, the Core Team, need to have a disaster plan in place in the event of unforeseen problems with the command and control of the Team. This is that disaster plan for the time being."

"I will let the Prime Minister, General Levy the Commander of the IDF, the Director of Mossad and the Director of the Kidon know about our plans and chain of command."

CHAPTER SIX

The next day, Jack spoke to General Levy, the Prime Minister, and the Director of the Kidon and laid out the process of Command for the Crossfire Team in any event. He tried to talk to Hiram Tzahal, the Director of the Mossad but could not reach him.

Two hours later he received a call from the Mossad directing him to meet with Director Tzahal at four p.m. that afternoon in the Director's office. Jack agreed to be there.

At three o'clock in the afternoon he sat down next to Laura and told her about his appointment. "I don't think it will take too long and I'll be back here around six p.m. or earlier.

Laura looked at her husband and put her hand in his. "You know, I am also concerned about the attacks of the enemy and the assassins roaming around looking to kill us. Do me a favor and wear your body armor under your clothes on this trip, okay?"

Jack grinned at her, "You think the Director of the Mossad isn't protected? Or, are you worried about me wandering around without you to protect me?"

She punched him in the arm. "Just wear it."

He agreed with her and looked around. They were the only two in the War Room at the moment. He pulled her up and hugged her. He kissed her on the lips and told her, "You know that I love you. But, did you know I also adore you? "I renewed your contract for another hundred years."

Laura grinned, "I know, I just took the eternity clause for you."

They laughed about it and discussed what they wanted to do for dinner after he got back.

As he got ready to go to the Mossad headquarters he realized that he had better wear his body armor or he'd catch it when he got back. So, he went to their apartment and put his body armor on and included two of the miniature video cameras to track his actions since he was going to have to explain to everybody whatever the Mossad Director would have to say anyway. The body armor included the cameras and their power source and they looked out at the neck level. He wore a turtle neck sweater to conceal the body armor so that he would not worry Director Tzahal. The cameras could see through the turtle neck material. He strapped on his .40 caliber XDM pistol in a flat pack on his right side under his sweater just in case he needed the firepower.

He went across the base and drove a power cart the quarter mile to the elevators. The elevator rose to the Portal level. He signed out of the base and had the Mossad issue him a driver and a car. It was one of the black Chevrolet Tahoe SUVs. It only took fifteen minutes to reach the Mossad Headquarters. The new rules required him to surrender his pistol at the guard post in the building. He went down, over, and down again in the elevator and walked to the Director's office. The Director's aide had him wait several minutes and then ushered him into the office.

Director Tzahal was behind his desk and rose to meet Jack as he entered.

Without warning, a demon manifested between the two men. It had its back to Jack and immediately stepped forward and ran his small black sword into Director Tzahal's chest and through his heart.

Jack had started praying as soon as the demon appeared and his armor and sword appeared. The demon disappeared back into the demonic dimension and the door behind Jack flew open in response to a shove by the aide and another Mossad agent.

Hiram Tzahal, the Mossad Director collapsed onto his desk in a bloody heap and the aide pointed a pistol at Jack as his armor faded out of sight. "Don't move or I will shoot!" the aide yelled for reinforcements.

Jack stood still in shock. Thinking about it he realized that to the men in the door it looked incriminating for Jack. He was standing there in his armor with his sword while the Director was collapsing with a sword wound through his heart. Considering the circumstances, he would have thought that he had killed the Director himself.

He started to pray to the Father and was surprised to see his armor and sword reappear. He heard in his mind, "Run!"

He turned around and the aide shot him twice. The bullets bounced off of his armor and he stepped forward and swung his sword which decapitated the Aide with one blow. The Aide's body fell to the floor and dissipated in greasy red smoke.

Jack grabbed the Mossad agent and he shimmered into a demon. Jack gutted the demon with his sword and it also dissipated into smoke and demon stain.

Jack noticed the closed door to the office and heard pounding footsteps on the other side of the door. He stepped back into the Director's office and closed and locked the door as his armor and sword disappeared.

He prayed that the Father would show him the emergency exit to the office because he was sure that anyone on the level of the Director of the Mossad would have one. He had a flash vision of a button on the underside of the main drawer on the Director's desk.

Jack stepped around the desk and found the button. He pushed it and one of the wall panels behind him opened up to a small elevator. Jack stepped into the elevator as first, the panel, and then the elevator door closed. The elevator quickly rose upward until it stopped and opened its door. A panel in the alley opened silently. Jack stepped out of the elevator and the door and panel silently closed again.

Jack looked around and quickly ran down the alley until he reached a cross street. He looked around and saw a bus approaching a stop. He ran to the bus stop and entered the bus. He had enough Israeli money and offered the driver a bill. The driver gave him the change and Jack sat down on the seat as the bus pulled away from the curb.

Up to this point Jack hadn't thought about what he was going to do next. He was just making sure he wasn't thrown into prison without a trial. The Mossad knew he was going to see Director Tzahal but wouldn't find him standing over the body.

He was sure that if he went back to the base he would be arrested by the Mossad team at the Portal for interrogation about the death of the Mossad Director. Satan had really set him up.

As the bus traveled its route Jack prayed for enlightenment and wisdom as to what he should do. He didn't want any of the anger of the Mossad due to the fact that he might be involved in the Director's being killed to attach itself to the Team. So, where would he go?

He sat there and realized there hadn't been enough time by the time he left to get the "burn phone" from Ethan and he was sure the Mossad could track his phone. He pulled out the phone, turned it off, and opened it up. He pulled out the SIM chip and broke it into pieces. He put them in his pocket to dispose of after he left the bus. Now he could try to find a pay phone and call the base. But, that would also be intercepted by the Mossad.

Now what?

CHAPTER SEVEN

Jack sat on the Tel Aviv bus and realized he had been in this situation before. He remembered when "Don" Miland had blamed the death of two Denver policemen on him and Laura. This was the same thing. Only there was four years of faith and combat against the devil since then. His confidence returned and he started to think clearly.

He remembered another time when he had saved two little girls for a mother in the northern desert of Israel and she had given him a phone number. His memory flew back to that time.

-----------------------******-----------------------

"After talking to the officer, Mrs. Jakobson walked over to the Malones. She stood there and looked at Laura and then at Jack. "My name is Iris Jakobson and I owe the two of you four times my life for saving my children for me. I was weak and you were strong for me. I will not forget it, ever. She slowly spelled out an international phone number. Jack memorized it immediately. She came over and pulled Jack's head down and gave him a kiss on the cheek and a hug. Looking up at his face she said, "Thank you." from the bottom of my heart. *If you ever need help, remember that number. Help will be there for you.*"

Iris Jakobson had been very grateful because Laura had rescued her son and daughter from a mine field and Jack had rescued her two other younger daughters from the terrorists who had just killed her husband.

-----------------------******-----------------------

Jack saw some stores coming up at the next corner and stood up and told the driver to let him out there. He stepped from the bus and went into a convenience store. He asked for a pay phone and converted a bill into change. He asked the store clerk how much a phone call was. The man didn't speak English but he showed Jack the correct change.

Jack put the change into the phone and called the number from the past. A man answered and Jack asked if he spoke English. The man spoke in Hebrew and left the phone for a few minutes. Then a woman answered the phone and said, "Can I help you?"

Jack smiled as he remembered her voice. "Iris Jakobson?"

She said, "Yes, this is Iris Jakobson, who is this?"

Jack replied, "Two years ago in the northern desert my wife and I saved your children. You told me to call you if I ever needed help."

There was a pause and Ms. Jakobson said, "Mr. Malone, how good of you to call me. I've thought about you and your wife many times. How can I help you?"

Jack thought about that. "I need a ride and a place to remain out of sight for a short time and I want to avoid any Mossad entanglements if possible."

There was a short pause and she said, "Where are you?"

Jack told her to wait a minute. He set the phone down and asked the clerk what the address was for the store. He picked up the phone and told her.

She said, "I will send a car for you. He will be there in about fifteen to twenty minutes. The license plate number ends in 354 and the car is a dark blue four door sedan."

Jack said, "Thank you."

Iris said, "Until we meet."

Jack bought a newspaper and stared at it while he waited. It was in Hebrew which he didn't know how to read, as yet. He stayed in the store and watched as a police car cruised by.

A dark blue sedan pulled into the parking lot of the store and the last three numbers on the plate were 354. Jack exited the store and got into the front passenger seat. He looked at the driver who smiled at him and drove out of the parking lot.

Thirty minutes later the car pulled into a gated community and then into a private gated home. Jack got out at the door and the driver moved the car to a garage.

The door opened on the house and Iris Jakobson came out and greeted Jack warmly. She led him into the house and into a large and lovely living room. Jack sat on a couch and she sat in a chair across from him. She smiled at him and asked him what in the world was going on.

Jack prayed for guidance and was pleased when the Father told him to tell the truth. So, he started from the time they had met in a small sand storm and hit the high points including their battles with demons up until he walked into her house.

She frowned and asked why he had fled from the Mossad headquarters since he had done no wrong.

Jack smiled, "I prayed and the Father in Heaven told me to run. I have to admit it didn't look good for me in Director Tzahal's office with the Director dead of a sword wound.

CHAPTER EIGHT

Iris Jakobson listened to Jack Malone's story about what happened in Hiram Tzahal's office and weighed the truth of it in her mind. She knew Jack was an honest man that had offered his own life to save her children. But, she didn't know if she believed him about the story of a demon killing the Director.

She looked at Jack. "Can you prove what you say are the facts about the Director's death?"

Jack understood her quandary. He prayed for guidance and suddenly remembered he did have proof of his innocence. "Have you got access to a computer here?"

She nodded in the affirmative. "Yes, I have several computers here."

Jack stood up and took off his sweater. His body armor was sort of a statement of its own. He asked her to show him a computer with a USB port. She got up and led him into another room in the house. It looked to be a home office. She showed him the computer. Jack disconnected a lead from the left side of his body armor. He connected the lead to the USB port on the computer and sat down. He typed in three commands and the screen lit up with a video. This showed him leaving the undersea base and travelling to the Mossad headquarters building and eventually entering the Director's office. He stopped the action and told her, "Understand, a spiritual being cannot be captured on video or by a camera. Therefore, you will not actually see the demon in this video."

She nodded her head. Jack started the video up again and the attached audio recorded the door closing behind him and the Director standing up with his hand out to greet Jack. Suddenly, while Jack was still ten feet from the Director blood appeared on the chest of the man and he clutched his chest and fell forward to the desk. The scene showed a golden glow and Jack's sword appeared to the right of the picture. It disappeared and the Aide could be heard yelling "Don't move or I will shoot!" The scene shifted as Jack turned around and faced the two men and his armor and sword reappeared.

Jack stepped toward the Aide who shot Jack twice and then graphically showed Jack decapitating the man who turned into a shimmering figure that coalesced into a smoke and dissipated. Then it showed Jack grabbing the other Mossad Agent and stabbing him also. He too became smoke.

The video showed Jack stepping back into the Director's office and shutting and locking the door. Jack stopped it there and disconnected the video leads.

He stood up and apologized to the older woman for having to let her see the three deaths in such graphic detail.

She thought about what she had seen. She looked at Jack and then led him back to the living room. After he had replaced his sweater and sat down he asked, "I believe that the whole meeting was a set up to incriminate me and to discredit either me or the Team with the Mossad."

She nodded her head. "Yes, I understand that. I also know that it was a set up because of the two demons that you killed who were imitating the Director's Aide and the other Mossad Agent. I also believe you because you needed to have a computer to show me the video. This is something that you could not have planned on in your flight. Would you trust me to help you resolve this matter?"

Jack smiled a small smile. "I trust you but I do not want you to become involved in my problems because you would probably be painted with the same brush and considered a co-conspirator of mine. Like I told you on the phone, I just needed a ride and a place that was out of sight so I could contact my wife at our base. With this video I should be able to convince the Mossad of my innocence."

About that time the man that had driven Jack to Ms. Jacobson's house knocked on the doorframe and waited to be allowed to interrupt the conversation. When she motioned him to come in he bent over and spoke quietly in her ear. He then straightened up and waited for her direction.

She nodded and he left the room. She looked at Jack and asked, "You said that your team was in conflict with assassins from this RHONE group?"

Jack nodded his head. "Yes, we fought with them several weeks ago in downtown Tel Aviv. Why?"

She frowned, "I think you may have been followed here. Charles tells me that there are several groups of men that have breached the community gates and are surrounding this house."

Jack shook his head. "Please, let me use your phone to see if we can get some help from our base? I should have guessed the demons would tell the assassins where I was and I should not have involved you in this matter. I am sorry and I ask you to forgive me for leading these villains to your home."

Iris nodded her head. "Come with me", she said as she quickly rose to her feet.

Jack followed her through her office and through a door he hadn't seen before when he was in the office. She went into the room which looked to be a converted laundry room and turned on the lights. She pressed a hidden switch under a cabinet to her left and three panels slid down to reveal weapons, lots of weapons. Jack looked at her and she made a small face and shrugged her shoulders slightly as if to apologize for not letting him know about this. "I saw that they took the weapon you had when you entered the Mossad headquarters building. Why don't you pick out a replacement and possibly a somewhat heavier weapon for the upcoming conflict?"

Somewhat bemused, Jack did as she said and then loaded both weapons with ammo. He took several extra magazines for the SOCOM FN SCAR Mark 17 CQC, a Close Quarters Combat Assault Rifle which used the heavier 7.62 MM round. He noticed that Iris had taken a baby Eagle pistol and another of the close quarters combat SCARs for herself. Each of the SCAR Mark 17s included the 40 MM grenade launcher. They both had grabbed a bandolier holding ten HE rounds for the grenade launchers. Iris replaced the panels with another push of a button and led the way out of the room.

As they left the room, Charles, the man who had spoken to her appeared and handed her some body armor and a helmet. He gave another helmet to Jack.

Jack smiled, "I get the impression that you are a lot more than you seem to be on the surface."

Iris nodded her head, "Yes, it would seem so." This was said as she loaded the first round into her SCAR.

As she finished she reached in her pocket and pulled out a cell phone. She handed it to Jack. "Here, make your call but warn whoever comes that there are friendlies in combat with these forces."

CHAPTER NINE

Jack dialed the number for COMM/SEC at the undersea base. Ethan answered with a neutral voice not recognizing the calling number. "Can I help you?"

Jack smiled, "Yes, you can Ethan, let me talk to Mark or Laura right away."

Ethan brightened up, "Yes Sir, General." Ten seconds later Jack heard Mark's voice. "Mark, I'll explain later but I am with a friend and her house is being surrounded by several dozen RHONE assassins and I could use some help."

Mark asked for his coordinates and Jack told him to lock onto the signal from the phone he was using. "Listen, there are Israelis that are on our side outside fighting the assassins, so don't just do a scorched earth approach. You'll know the bad guys by the fact that they will be the ones firing on you."

Mark came back with, "Ten-Four, we are less than three minutes away and loaded for bear. Connelly out."

Jack handed the phone back to Iris and nodded. "We've got more backup coming and it is the best kind."

She nodded and turned to leave the building. Jack put his hand on her shoulder, stopping her. "Listen Iris, this group of assassins is working under the control of several demons. If we get the upper hand on the assassins there could be a demon intervention. If that happens, have your people fire on the demons once. If they have not gotten Yahveh's permission to be here, your bullets will kill them. If they are in our dimension legally and your bullets don't bother them, then let me or my people deal with them, understand? Can you tell your people that?"

See looked at Jack and nodded. She spoke into a hidden microphone embedded into her body armor to warn someone. Jack was amazed at everything this lady was doing.

About that time there was a crash off to the left of Jack's position and he quickly headed that way. Iris was talking to her microphone again and right on Jack's heels.

Stopping and peering around a corner Jack saw three men stepping through a busted back door. They were all armed with assault rifles. Jack quickly stepped over to the other side of the opening, while he opened up on the intruders with his SCAR. 7.62 MM rounds slammed into all three men with some of the rounds hitting them in the head. As they fell back or down, one of dead men triggered his M-16 and burned through the twenty round magazine stitching holes in the walls and the ceiling.

Two more of the assassins started shooting through the open back door and Iris ripped off half a magazine from her SCAR. She hit one man and he went down. The other man retreated out of sight. There was a sudden explosion and the man's body flew through the Kitchen window in a bloody mess with glass being blown all over the kitchen. As he and Iris ducked back from the explosion Jack commented to Iris, "Mark's here."

Iris's associate, Charles, suddenly ran past Iris and Jack and threw himself to the floor and slid between the two assassin's bodies and threw two grenades out of the broken door. He covered up and Jack and Iris moved back around the corners until the mini-bombs exploded outside. The man on the floor jumped up and went out the door with his rifle firing.

Jack had seen that type of action before and looked at Iris. "Kidon?"

She nodded her head. She motioned Jack back toward the front of the house. Jack stayed alert but the action outside was quickly dying off. Jack safed his rifle and waited. There was a knock on the front door and Iris walked up and opened the door to admit Mark Connelly and Laura. Both were in full battle dress and carrying M-8s with smoke rolling off of their barrels.

Iris asked them to come into her home and hugged Laura which was somewhat awkward since both of them had on body armor and were holding rifles. Laura looked at Jack with a raised eyebrow about Iris. Jack smiled and shrugged his shoulders.

The combined Mossad, Kidon, and Crossfire Team finished cleaning up outside the home and settled in as a line of defense around the house.

After everyone in the front room had set the safeties their rifles and set them down, they retired to the living room. Everyone was introduced and seated. Jack looked at Iris and asked, "Would you care to explain your interesting dual nature to us?"

Iris thought for a few moments and then nodded. "You deserve an explanation. In my daily life, I am, or rather was, the Senior Assistant Director of the Mossad. I believe I am now the new Director, pending approval by the Prime Minister."

Jack shook his head and laughed. "And I called you and told you I didn't want any Mossad entanglements. You must have thought I was more than a little crazy."

Iris grinned and made a small face. "I was surprised when you called but decided it would be a good time to clear the air while you were unaware of my relationship with the Mossad."

Iris smiled at Jack. "Don't let it worry you, Jack. I already knew you did not kill Hiram." She saw the question on his face. "You must understand that you are not the only ones with video cameras. We didn't see the demon but I wanted your explanation without having to detain you. That worked out quite well, considering."

Jack nodded, "I do want to give you my condolences for the death of Director Tzahal and I appreciate your "helping" me in what I thought was a time of need. Also, I believe now that the Father had me run so that I would re-encounter you."

Iris looked inward and then tentatively smiled. "You believe that the reason you were there when the demon killed my old friend was because YHVH wanted us to become reacquainted?"

Jack nodded, "Iris, I don't pretend to understand Yahveh and how he orchestrates people and events. I can tell you that His thoughts and ways are much higher than our thoughts and ways. A year and a half ago we were tasked to stop a deranged man from Texas, in the United States, who had been led by demons to think Israel had killed his U. S. Air Force pilot son whom he idolized. This multi-billionaire raised a small army and stole and launched three U.S. Trident nuclear missiles at Israel."

Iris nodded, "I am aware of that event."

Jack continued, "We, the Crossfire Team, had hunted him and his mercenaries down and destroyed the remnants of his army plus his control center in Texas. But we were too late. His people had already launched the missiles. There was absolutely nothing on Earth that could stop those MIRVed warheads from totally destroying this country. The missiles had reached apogee, or their highest point in their arc, before they would come down on Israel. At that exact split second of time a small bunch of meteors that had been roaming through space for millions of years entered our atmosphere and destroyed all three of the missiles. Not only that, one small meteor became a meteorite and struck the Earth exactly at the place and where the car of the billionaire who was attempting to escape the hand of God was moving."

"I am now fairly certain that the death of Director Tzahal was woven into a part of God's plan that also reunited us. God never misuses his children. I believe that the Director's death was the best possible future he had. That is why I think this is all a part of God's plan. That and the fact that both Satan and the RHONE want our guts for garters and God allowed them to engineer everything so that we could meet again. Are you sure you want to remain acquainted with myself and the Crossfire Team?"

She smiled, "Absolutely, your God is my G-d, and I will leave my protection in His hands. You people are the only ones I know of who are an anointed defense against these demons from Satan. But, that makes you definitely a major magnet to draw trouble of all kinds. I want our two organizations to work closely together so that we can help resolve these types of problems for the State of Israel."

"You don't resolve problems by avoiding them. I would like to suggest that since you have made Israel your home you might want to learn the language and the Jewish way of doing things. This would allow G-d to bless each of you with even more protection and possibly enrich your lives."

"I can now see that YHVH has anointed you and your team to do battle against the human and spiritual enemies of our country. That includes all of you also as this is now your country. But it would be wise for you to fully join the Jewish people and become the apple of G-d's eye for all time. As Judea-Christians you are a part of the family of

Israel. And, for your information, this suggestion is a word that G-d just dropped into my spirit for you all. Be blessed, Shalom."

CHAPTER TEN

They all thanked Iris for her assistance and Jack left with the rest of the team in the helicopter to return to the Sea Base.

Upon their arrival Jack gave his videos and his after-action report to Ethan for recording. He went to his apartment since it was almost midnight. He showered and the climbed into bed next to Laura and gave her a reassuring kiss and a gentle hug. She smiled in her sleep and he quickly fell asleep. Early the next morning he went to the War Room to catch up on what had been going on in his absence.

While wrapped up in his work Jack sensed someone standing quietly to his right. He looked over and saw Elon, their newest employee.

Jack grinned at the younger man. "You know; you should not sneak up on people like that around here. It could be harmful to your health even if you are a former Kidon agent."

Elon grinned, "All right, I will try to stop doing it, although it's a hard habit to break. You have to admit that you didn't notice me until I was next to you, did you?"

Jack shook his head, "No, I didn't notice you. But, as I explained to you earlier, we work as a team." As he turned back to his work he used his thumb and motioned behind Elon.

Elon turned to look and found Laura standing there quietly with her handgun loosely pointed at him. He realized he hadn't heard her either. "Point taken; Hello Laura."

Laura holstered her weapon and smiled, "Hello Elon."

Jack asked over his shoulder, "I take it that you had a reason for sneaking up on me other than to see if you could surprise me?"

Elon nodded his head. "Yes, I wanted to tell you about some scuttlebutt I heard from my Kidon mates late last night. It seems that someone in the Mossad was telling others that you had killed the Director of the Mossad and disappeared. My first thought was that you would not do something like that."

"But the Mossad Collections Agent was adamant in his statement. Two of the Kidon laughed at him and told him that not only did you not do that, but you had killed two demons that were part of a plot against the Director. The Mossad Agent then said that wasn't true because demons weren't real. That really got a laugh out of the Kidon. They seriously invited him along on the next combined outing we have."

Jack laughed, "Thank you Elon for that information. You're right, I wouldn't kill the Director unless God told me to do it and He doesn't trifle around with His children that way. How is your new job going?"

Elon relaxed and smiled. "Very well, thank you. The teams of the SOG that you gave me are hitting all of their marks. I also have to admit that I have learned a great deal about things that I thought I already knew from the lessons that You, Mark, Laura, and Sarah have been teaching. However, I'm not sure that I will survive my Martial Arts lessons with Su Li, but I'm trying."

Jack nodded, "You should compare notes with Ethan about your Martial Arts training. I think you two will find you have a lot in common there." Jack made a mental note to talk to Su Li about the fear she was instilling in her students.

Elon asked, "I understand most of the things I am being taught but why are you teaching me sword fighting?"

Jack stopped working and turned around to face the young Israeli. He grinned, "Because all of the people in your team are already God's sword bearers and are anointed to fight demons. You didn't think that you will get to sit on the sidelines forever did you?" As you have already given your life to Yahveh and Yahshua and you are one of us, therefore you are a candidate for God's anointing to be a sword bearer."

After Elon left Jack went back to work on his responsibilities until the COMM/SEC technician told him that he had an incoming call from Iris, the Director of the Mossad.

Jack picked up the phone and touched the button for that line. "Hello, Director, how can I help you today?"

Iris Jakobson bid him hello and asked how he had managed after the night before. Then she said, "I just wanted to let you know that the autopsy on my predecessor generated an interesting fact. He had an aneurism that was about to burst in his brain. The Medical Examiner told me that it was a miracle that the man had lived long enough to die from a sword blade thrust through his heart. The Examiner also said curiously that his examination showed no brain activity just before the sword hit his body. The entire medical team and the Medical Examiner can't understand why but they swear that the facts indicate that he died peacefully just before the demon appeared. You were right, that was the best path he had ahead of him."

Jack concurred, "God loves each one of us more than we could ever imagine. I believe that your predecessor's spirit left this earth before the demon attacked him. Iris, I pray that your future as Director of the Mossad will be stellar and God will back you all the days of your life."

Iris said, "Thank you Jack, I wish the same for you and I would like you and Laura to meet with me this afternoon."

After he hung up the call Jack thought about the request from Iris. Then he called Mark. "Hey, buddy, what are you up to right now?"

Mark laughed, "I was trying to figure out a schedule of realistic drills for the entire membership of the team so that we can stay on top of our alert requirements. I'm thinking of having Aaron and Judah dress up as demons again so it adds realism to the alert."

Jack thought about that. "You have a problem with that. Even though they look realistic our armor and swords won't appear because they are not real demons."

Mark sighed, "That's right. Oh well, what did you need?"

Jack told Mark that he and Laura had been requested to go to the office of the new Director of the Mossad this afternoon and give her an update on the battle with the RHONE and I want you to be in charge while I am gone."

That afternoon Jack and Laura went to the Mossad headquarters building. The strange elevator was familiar now and they were ushered into Iris Jakobson's office on time.

Iris was glad to see them and hugged them both. Jack was somewhat concerned after what had happened the last time he came to this office and he suggested that they pray for protection from the enemy of all men. They prayed to the God of Abraham, Isaac, and Jacob with the Director.

Laura told her about the recent wedding of David Zahavy and Alexis Hutton and suggested that when she got a break in her workload as Director that she make a trip to the base and they would have a party to celebrate her new position.

As they headed back to the base, Laura commented on the fact that Iris looked like she was under a lot of strain and it was taxing her somewhat. Jack had noticed the stress and suggested they pray for God's peace to fill her. After praying they arrived at the Portal. When they reached the Crossfire Team side of the base they went to the War Room, and worked on paperwork and some filing that was piling up.

Jack finished his paperwork and began to pray about Iris's suggestion about them becoming involved in the Jewish traditions and lifestyle. In the midst of his prayer the angel Rose appeared to both him and Laura. Rose was in her fierce white and muted gold colors. She looked at and through them. Then she spoke in a quiet voice, for her, and told them. *"I am glad that you have started to heed the Mossad Director's suggestion. Because, it was more than a suggestion as far as Yahveh is concerned.*

Rose's last statement as she faded out stayed with Jack. She had quietly said, *"The Father wants to bless you more than he can in many areas. It would be much easier if you would understand and celebrate His appointed times while you are living here with His chosen people. Speak to David and Sarah."*

Jack used the combat communications net to call David Zahavy and Sarah and have them come to the War Room.

Laura looked at Jack with a worried or at least, very concerned expression. "What "appointed times" are we not doing?" Jack shook his head. He wasn't sure. He looked up as David, Alexis, Sarah, and Mark walked into the War Room.

David spoke up. "Is it all right if Alexis and Mark sit in this meeting?"

Jack nodded, "They need to hear this anyway."

Thinking better of the arrangements with this many people Jack suggested they adjourn to the large conference room across the way from the War Room.

After everyone was seated and comfortable Jack reminded everyone of the Mossad Director's suggestion and he repeated Rose's comments that Yahveh wanted them to do observe His Appointed Times.

David smiled, "Don't let this worry you. Because you grew up in a Gentile home, you were not granted a heritage of Judaism. While this may seem like an insurmountable challenge, it is not that bad at all. What you are talking about is the Jewish Roots of Jesus. He was a practicing Jew from His birth until He ascended into Heaven. I can tell you what you've missed and how to correct it. But, first, you need some background so that it will all make sense."

"Understand that many of these are deeply imbedded Jewish traditions founded thousands of years ago. But, these are traditions based on the word of YHVH and codified by Jewish leaders. They have been followed for centuries because they work and they are real. They all honor the God of the Universe and bring His blessings."

CHAPTER ELEVEN

David smiled again. "The history of the schism between Jews and Christians started with the Council of Nicaea in the middle of the third century. Constantine wanted to control Christianity and he knew he had to divorce the new religion, Christianity, from the established religion of Judaism to solidify his domination.

The Jews wouldn't hear of Constantine's rule over Judaism and he was well aware of the stubbornness of the Hebrew race. There was a natural dislike between Jews who believed that Yahshua was the Messiah and those in charge of Judaism at that time who could not allow belief in Yahshua. The leaders denounced Yahshua and came down hard on anyone who followed "the way".

"Over the next two thousand years' anti-Semitism reared its repulsive head as people feared the Jews and their God. In the last two centuries the devil fanned the flames of hatred against the Jews for many reasons. The prime one was that the Jewish race is the favorite of the God of Abraham, Isaac, and Jacob. And Israel is His chosen land for His chosen people. Lately, in the Christian Church, "replacement theology" has been the chosen path for many Christians. It speaks to the concept that because the Jews rejected Jesus Christ that God has eliminated them as the chosen people and replaced them with the Christians."

"Nothing could be further from the truth. Because the Jews rejected Yahshua (Jesus), God grafted the new believers into the faith and both Theologies were supposed to study and pray next to each other. The Bible states that in the last days, God will bless a group of Gentiles so greatly that the Jews will become envious and return to worshiping Yahveh. It is the "Latter Rain" talked about in the Bible. God has a plan to bring his chosen people back to Him through faith in His Son, Yahshua."

"But, because of the concerted effort of the anti-Semitism the two systems compete against each other and in truth, over the centuries the Christians have enslaved, attacked and tried to destroy Jews from the Crusades to

Hitler and the Holocaust. But, God has a plan and it will come about. Now, you are grafted into the Jewish faith through your acceptance of Yahshua. Lately, there are Christian Churches and Ministries that are teaching the "Jewish Roots of Jesus" and repairing the world through creating the one new man with both Jew and Gentile roots. This is based in "Tikkun olam" (in Hebrew, תקון or תיקון עולם עולםwhich is a Hebrew phrase that means "repairing the world" (or "healing the world") which suggests humanity's shared responsibility to heal, repair and transform the world. In Judaism, the concept of *tikkun olam* originated in the early rabbinic period. The concept was given new meanings in the Kabbalah of the medieval period and has come to possess further connotations in modern Judaism."

"God is waking up Gentiles and they are learning to apply the Jewish Roots to their lives and are seeing incredible new Revelation as they open themselves up to the God of Abraham, Isaac, and Jacob."

Jack thought about the Jewish Roots and how they applied to himself and the others around him. He looked at David, "How many things about our Jewish Roots do we need to learn immediately? We're already celebrating Shabbat and Havdalah."

David thought for a minute. "There are fourteen more things you need to adopt so that you can get a sense of how Yahveh God wants to interface with you on a daily basis. I am going to give you an item and a short explanation of it. As you begin to practice all of these things they will become natural and easy to do on a daily basis. Believe me, when I tell you, after you experience the blessings of Yahveh simply because you honor Him by doing these things, you will yearn to do them properly and with great joy."

David smiled at Sarah and said to everyone. "There are things in this list that are good to start now, but, you should continually grow in your relationship with God and the Scriptures for the rest of your life. People, you need to forget the labels of Jewish and Christian and remember that we both study the same Old Testament of the Bible. In those pages are God's instructions for His people. That is who you are! You are God's people and you need to obey what He told His people to do. These commandments and instructions are His desired methods of communication and dedication to Him by His People."

"First thing you want to do is to joyfully celebrate Shabbat, to welcome in the Sabbath, as you have been doing. Do it every Friday that you can. The second item is to celebrate Havdalah, which marks the end of each Shabbat or other holidays, which you are also doing presently. Do that every Saturday if possible."

"The next thing will be to study Torah. The Torah is the first five books of the Old Testament. There are so many levels of revelation in the Torah that many Rabbis and scholars study Torah their entire lives and every day they are learning new things as God gives them Revelation from His word. We have created, here in the Sea Base, a Judeo-Christian prayer and faith center. We still need a Torah knowledgeable study leader. We need to quickly find a Rabbi for that position. How is the search going?"

Jack nodded, "We want to host a Messianic-Jewish Rabbi as our teacher and as someone who could handle corporate spiritual matters, like the correct celebration of the "Appointed Times" or the "Festivals" for the Team."

David laughed, "First you need to understand a basic misunderstanding about the "Appointed Times" and the "Festivals". These things are God's Appointed times and His Festivals, and while they are celebrated universally by those of the Jewish faith they are not "Jewish" things. God gave them to all Men to follow before the Jewish people were a people. Also, you'd better find a Rabbi that can handle the very active spiritual life that this group enjoys. He also needs to be able to handle the concept of demons in our dimension."

Jack nodded, "So true David, so true. That gives me an idea. I'll go talk to Rabbi Simon ben Chanan. He is very likely knowledgeable as to who is available and qualified as Rabbis for us to interview. He also clearly understands the demonic angle."

Sarah looked at Jack. "You need to understand that most Jewish Rabbis are intolerant of Rabbis that believe in Yahshua. Violently some times. Will Rabbi Chanan help you find a non-Jewish-only Rabbi?"

Jack shrugged, "Abba was the one that gave me the thought to seek Rabbi Chanan for help in this matter."

David said, "I see that many of the Team are wearing and using the Tallit during prayer. That is good. Do you all understand that is the prayer shawl that Yahshua wore while he was on Earth? It is your private prayer closet and the enemy cannot interfere or overhear you while you use it."

Since we haven't started Torah studies yet I want to introduce you to another "God" thing. The Mezuzah literally means "doorpost". It is a small case, attached to the doorposts of dwellings, which contains a scroll with passages of scripture written on it. There are special procedures and prayers for affixing the mezuzah. You place one on every doorpost, except for the bathroom, and acknowledge the scriptures whenever you pass through the door associated with that Mezuzah, God will bless you with divine protection and bless the works of your hands, whether going in or going out."

"Now, there are seven Feasts you celebrate each year. Three of them are "Appointed Times" which you come to the Lord and you don't come empty-handed. The three Feasts are Passover, Pentecost, and Sukkot. These are the three holidays that you bring your "First Fruits" offering to the Lord. We'll cover all of that as we go through the year."

"You and your troops are already aware of paying your Tithe or ten-percent each Sabbath and the Charity box or Tzdakah box. If you learn about, understand, and adopt these things then you will understand the Jewish people and their daily connection with Yahveh and He can bless you fully. Remember, to the Jews this not a "religion", it is a complete way of life.

CHAPTER TWELVE

Two days later Jack answered a call from Ethan. "Hello Ethan, what's going on?"

Ethan was jumbling his words together in an attempt to get his message to Jack in the shortest time.

Jack told him to slow down, take a deep breath and then tell him what the problem was.

Ethan did as he was told and then said, "Jack, I have just gotten an emergency call from the Mossad that their headquarters is under attack by unknown forces and there is a demonic element to the attack. They are requesting our immediate assistance. What do I tell them?"

Jack said, "hit the All Team Alarm and then respond to the Mossad and tell them that the Crossfire Team is on the way."

As the alarms sounded and the personnel started to grab their armor and weapons, Jack and Laura ran to the armory and got their gear on. Mark ran into the armory already dressed for war. He saw Jack and hurried over to him. "I haven't heard from Carol about this and she should have seen it in the Matrix. I'll bet the assault is a trap for us. I've passed that on to the Crossfire Air Force and they will be flying cover for us. Let's arrange our troops so that we don't all get blindsided if this is a trap."

Laura had finally gotten Carol on her combat comm set. "What is going on Carol? We're being told that there is an assault on the Mossad headquarters and there are demons involved. Did you see anything in the Matrix about this?"

Carol ran into the armory talking on her phone to Laura, "No, I looked at it less than twenty minutes ago and there were no demons scheduled to interface with our troops at all." She waved at Laura and put her phone down and dressed quickly in her battle armor and took her sniper rifle and ammo and ran toward the air field.

Jack and Mark quickly planned out their counter assault with a large backup force in the event it was simply a trap.

David got dressed and called General Levy. "General, do you have anything on a mixed warrior and demon assault on the Mossad headquarters building?"

General Levy said, "I've just been notified about it. My forces will be there in ten minutes."

David told him that the Crossfire Team would also be there about that time.

As everyone ran for the airfield Jack called the Director's office in the Mossad headquarters but got no answer. He shook his head and jumped onto the ramp of the V22 Osprey as it was starting to take off. He clambered into the body of the craft and found Laura sitting in one of the jump seats. He handed her his rifle as he ran up to the flight deck.

Su Li was piloting the aircraft and Jack moved her earphone on her right side. "We need to be careful and look out for Man Pad weapons. This could be an elaborate trap by the RHONE."

Su Li nodded her head and shouted back over the noise of the engines, "Mark told me that Mike and two Mossad pilots are going in ahead of us in AH-1Z Super Cobra attack helicopters."

Jack gave her a thumbs up sign and headed back to the seats as the Tilt Rotor raced out of the tunnel and turned left over the city directly toward the Mossad headquarters. Su Li dropped the VH22 almost to street level as they neared the building and they could see explosions and troops fighting on the ground. Suddenly there were eight explosions on the rooftops of buildings near the headquarters as the Super Cobras took out several enemy troops with shoulder-mounted missiles who had been waiting for the Ospreys.

Su Li set the Osprey down on the street and the ramp was already open. The troops exited and formed up in assault squads. They moved on the headquarters building and had covered two blocks when there was an explosion behind them. Jack looked back and saw one wing and the back of the Osprey had been blown off of the aircraft which was doing a death dance as the other engine with its spinning blades fell to the street and the blades shattered. The force of the impact spun the aircraft around in a circle.

Jack prayed that God would protect Su Li and continued to move toward their target.

They were moving from cover to cover when they came under fire from ground troops spread out near the headquarters building. Everyone began returning fire and made progress in knocking down the enemy. Jack's combat comm system registered a call from General Levy. He answered it.

General Levy told Jack that the IDF was mopping up the ground troops outside the fake façade of the building but some of the enemy troops had gotten into the building and there were some demons keeping the IDF forces out of the building.

Jack detailed eight people to follow him as he ran for the main entrance. Jack got a word from the Lord and slid into the recessed doorway as rifle fire smacked into the building on both sides of the doorway.

He turned to the people with him and found Laura and Sarah, Megan, and five female members of the SOG. He told them, "Watch each other's back. I still think this is one of the assassins' traps."

CHAPTER THIRTEEN

Jack stepped around the smashed-in door and headed for the stairs assuming that the elevators wouldn't be working. As he came across the entryway two demons appeared and ran at the troops. Jack fired his rifle at the demons but it didn't affect them. He started to pray his combat prayer and his armor and sword appeared and he advanced on the demon running at him.

The demon swung its large black sword in a major slash at Jack. Jack parried the blow and the demon's sword shattered on the bright blade. Jack reversed his blow and came up from the bottom of the demon and cut its leading leg off and part of its body. The demon screamed in frustration but dissolved into black smoke. Laura and one of the SOG women had sliced and diced the second demon and everyone was advancing on the stairs again.

Jack had them hunker down and cover the stairwell door as he pulled it open. There weren't any demons or enemy soldiers in the stairwell so Jack started down toward the fifth lower level where the Director's office was. Most of his troops followed him while three of them stayed there and watched their back track.

Reaching the fifth floor door Jack looked out of the door as he cracked it open. There were only emergency lights shining and the darkness was oppressive. Jack reached up and pulled his NVGs down over his eyes. He could now see everything in shades of green. He slipped out of the stairwell and into the main aisle. He used hand signs to spread out the troops with him. He made a quick dash down the aisle to the cross aisle the Director's office was on. He and Laura were accompanied by Megan and one of the SOG women. Jack reached the office and told the others to wait just outside as he checked to see if there was anybody in the office. He opened the anteroom door and didn't see anybody. He slipped over to the door to the inner office and found it locked. He knocked on the door and waited.

A female voice asked who it was that had knocked. Jack said, "Crossfire Team, Jack Malone."

The door was unlocked and Iris peeked out at Jack. "Thank God you got here."

Jack nodded, "We can get you out of here if that is what you want to do."

She nodded and slipped out of the office and locked the door again. They moved over to the outer door and opened it. Laura saw them and smiled at Iris. Laura moved aside so that the Director and Jack could exit the room. Jack told Iris to stay with Megan and slipped back to the front of their little group. His comm sounded and he heard Mark's voice. "Jack, this is Mark, watch out if you're coming back to the front door. It is a battlefield right now. We've teamed up with the IDF and are reducing the enemy but there are still a bunch of them firing on the building."

Jack asked, "What the heck is this all about? There were two demons inside but the Director is with us."

Mark was silent for a second. "Jack, Iris Jakobson is out here with us."

Jack turned around in time to see the woman he had believed to be Iris shimmer and transform into a sleek demon who was raising its thin, black sword to kill Laura. Jack snap aimed his M-8 and shot the demon three times in the head. While the bullets didn't kill the demon, the impact of the bullets knocked the demon backward. This alerted everyone at the same time. Jack began to pray and his armor and sword appeared as he dropped his rifle on its lanyard. He sprang toward the demon to try and block the sword the demon was again trying to use on Laura. But, before he could cover the distance a bright shining blade came out of the demon's chest. The demon screamed a hideous noise and started dissolving into rank smoke. Jack watched as Megan appeared behind the vanishing demon resheathing her sword.

"Everyone start praying and then keep your armor and sword in operation. The demons are attempting to imitate normal humans. Check those around you and kill any demons you find. They won't let you approach them while your sword is active." He switched to Mark's number. "Megan dispatched our fake Iris. We're heading back to you now. We will come out the south door instead of the main east entrance." Mark agreed with the move.

They moved back to the stairwell and Jack called up to the reserve troops watching their back track. Nothing had happened so far. He sent the team up two at a time in the event the stairwell was compromised.

All eight of them made it to the south doorway and carefully eased out of the building and looked for the enemy. There were only random shots being fired and they couldn't see any of the enemy troops. Jack called Mark and told him they were out of the building.

Mark came back, "We've got Director Jakobson into the hands of General Levy and are mopping up out here. I think the battle is over and I'm still not sure of why they were attacking the Mossad headquarters. Watch your six and move back toward the Osprey and see if Su Li is all right. We'll move that way also."

Jack and Laura moved from cover to cover until they met a large force of the IDF. After each side was confident of the other forces identity, Jack and his smaller team ran back toward the still burning wreck of the Osprey.

Jack set four of the SOG troops as a perimeter guard as he and the others searched the wreckage for Su Li. Jack climbed up the side of the aircraft and looked into the cockpit. There was no body in there. Jack tried the comm again but didn't get anything from Su Li. He called Mike White in his Super Cobra and asked him to do an air search for the Asian pilot.

Jack suddenly got a call from the IDF. "General Malone? We've got your pilot here and she's a little banged up, but she's holding her own. We are halfway between the wreck of the Tilt Rotor and the interstate. Stay there and we'll bring her to you.

A few minutes later five IDF troops showed up with a bandaged Su Li. Jack thanked them and helped her back to where Laura and the others were standing guard.

Su Li sighed and spoke in a dull monotone voice, "I'm really tired right now, Jack."

Jack could see that. He had Laura check her over. Laura gave her some water from her canteen. Then she got Su Li to lie down on the grass. Laura called Jack over and stepping away she talked quietly to him.

Looking back at the smaller woman Laura said, "After the missile destroyed the plane it collapsed and spun around. Su Li managed to crawl out of the cockpit through the shattered windscreen. This was after the plane had stopped spinning. She's got some scrapes and cuts but I can't find anything broken or major bruising. She's clotted up and isn't bleeding anymore, but I'm worried about her. She is not acting normal. I think we need to pray and ask the Father to heal her. Jack, I'm _really_ worried about her."

Jack nodded and got several of the other Team members to pray healing for Su Li. Jack prayed a deep prayer for the Master of the universe to heal the young Asian woman.

Su Li cried out weakly and suddenly convulsed and shook. She fell back and didn't move. Laura knelt at her side and felt for a pulse. She could not find one and she cried out to God.

Jack told their med tech to start CPR and get a vehicle to transport Su Li to the nearby hospital. Before anyone could move there was a bright flash of light and Su Li vanished, Jack stood there and realized that there was nothing he could do. But, he still felt full of awe and joy in the Lord as he saw the hand of the Most High in everything that had happened. He just knew that Su Li would survive this latest attack of the enemy. He gathered in his wife and held her as she cried. He quietly told her to trust God; that everything was going to be all right.

CHAPTER FOURTEEN

Within the next twenty minutes the rest of the Crossfire troops arrived back to the wreck and settled down on the ground. They were dirty, sweat stained and exhausted. Other than Su Li there weren't any seriously wounded or dead troops but Jack could tell that they were all pretty well spent after three hours of fighting RHONE troops, demons, and trying not to get killed.

Jack negotiated with the Mossad and they brought in another V22 which landed close to the wreck. Everyone climbed on board and the aircraft took off and then loitered for ten minutes until there was no satellite coverage. They flew into the approach tunnel under the island and finally landed at the Sea Base.

Everyone was worried about Su Li and gathered in the living room in front of the War Room for a communal prayer. After that they cleaned up themselves and their weapons, they each did an after action report. Then it was time for an early bed call for most of the Team.

The Core Team gathered around Jack and Laura and asked about Su Li. Jack shook his head, "I don't know for sure but I do know she's in Heaven. Whether or not she will be back here being up to the Father and the Son. I don't have a heavy heart and actually feel very optimistic about our short but feisty friend."

Jack asked Carol to hang around as the other Core Team members left. She stood there and waited quietly. Jack sighed, 'Carol I'm concerned about the information in the Matrix about this battle. I shot two demons and it did not affect them. That means they had Yahveh's permission to be a part of this battle. Yet the Matrix did not show that information, right?"

Carol nodded, "I checked it just before the alert and there were no demons involved with the Crossfire Team on the information presented by the Matrix."

Jack thought for a few seconds. "Okay, I want you to go back and check it again before I start praying about this."

Carol nodded again. "All right." She walked over and got down on her knees and started praying. The white diamonds at her throat and forehead blazed into being.

Jack sat down to wait. Carol's diamonds faded out and she got up and walked over to where he was still in the act of sitting down. "I carefully checked the information on the Matrix. There are still no demons that were requested to do combat with our team. So I asked to speak to Hugo. He reviewed everything I did and then did his own search. He said that perhaps Satan asked for demons to attack the Mossad and they battled with us simply as a side action to their authorized attack. But, he could not find anywhere a request for demons that attacked our team. I think that is the first time I've seen Hugo perplexed. He told me that he would talk to the Most High to determine what happened. I told him that there were twenty-two demons that fought with various team members. He shook his head and told me that "This is a new thing." And, the next thing I knew, here I am."

Jack speculated, "Either Satan did not get God's approval for these demons but got them in our dimension with their characteristics still in effect, or he altered the Matrix so that they couldn't be seen. I think it is probably the latter because God is not mocked and his commands concerning demons entering our dimension are ironclad and not subject to debate or ignoring by Satan."

Carol nodded her head, "I think you could be right. I'll wait until I hear what Hugo has to tell me before I trust the information on the Matrix again."

CHAPTER FIFTEEN

Jack went to his apartment and dropped into one of the couches in the sitting room next to Laura who was seeking comfort in the Bible concerning Su Li.

He told her what Carol had found out and what Hugo had told her. "I am concerned that Satan is going to defy Yahveh God and that will change everything we do if that is the case.

Laura reached over and put her hand on his arm. "Honey, remember that God is Omnipotent and Satan cannot defy him without it costing him everything. I had a thought while I was praying for Su Li and I don't think it was my thought. I normally don't have thoughts like this one. You do and it works for you."

Jack grinned at her, "Okay, what was the thought?"

"I thought that if Satan did defy God enough to really make Him mad it would be a little thing for God to rewrite all history and time and eliminate Satan completely. He would never have existed."

Jack looked at her, "WOW! That is true, God could do that. If he did, we would not remember Satan but it would be some other fallen angel that turned evil but was willing to do things God's way. That hurts my brain to try to think about what would change in the six-thousand-year history of mankind."

Laura thought for a minute. "What if God has already done that, even seven times? If he kept the name, the same we'd never know if he changed out the character."

Jack shook his head, "That is just too deep for me to consider."

They gave up on the suppositions and Jack took a shower and they crawled into bed for some badly needed sleep.

Sometime later Jack woke with a start. There was someone other than Laura and himself in the bedroom. Jack opened his eyes and dimly saw Raquel standing at the foot of their bed. Jack reached over and gently shook Laura awake. "We've got company."

Raquel was apparently involved with something other than just communicating to Jack and Laura. After roughly thirty seconds he took a deep breath and focused on them.

Jack turned on the bedside light. "Good evening Raquel, what is your mission tonight?"

Raquel was in his jeans and plaid shirt version. "Greetings Jack and Laura, I bring you news of your team mate Su Li. She is sleeping back in her room and is completely healthy. She won't remember her trip to Heaven because she was not supposed to be there in God's plan. The RHONE soldier that fired on her aircraft had already been killed by the helicopters. Satan reanimated him so that he could shoot his missile at the plane. It was only because Satan contravened God's laws and His commandments that Su Li died. So the Father has restored her to life and returned her to you so that she can serve Him."

The Archangel smiled at the two humans. "I was present when the Most High took Satan to task for violating that rule and for ignoring God's laws and introducing demons into the human dimension without permission. Satan will not do that again, ever. You have God's word on that. We angels have never seen Satan so frustrated. I think, as your people would say, that you drove him insane. There is a new agreement between Satan and God that will limit Satan's ability to affect the human dimension greatly. I know it will not mean much to you, but Satan no longer has the ability to use the seventh and eight dimensions."

"I hope that you will understand that God created everyone, even Satan. But, his pride makes him act like an unruly child. Satan has to learn to control his outbursts and do things God's way." Raquel winked at the couple and faded out of sight.

Laura sighed, "Now we'll never know if my idea was right or not." Jack said, "Rest assured honey, we wouldn't have known anyway." Jack sent a text to all the people on the Crossfire Team with the exception of Su Li, advising them about God's intervention in Su Li's life and death.

The next morning was hectic as the after action reports had to be completed. That morning the Osprey that had been destroyed suddenly appeared completely normal at the Mossad Helipad by the Portal before 5 a.m.

Ethan Reaper walked into the War Room and smiled at the commanding couple. "I have to tell you that it must have been a good trip to heaven for her. I think God took away her anger or something. She's just as strict and wants great results but it's now strictly a training and she doesn't act like she's dissatisfied with me or anybody else if we don't do it right. She actually took me aside and showed me how to correct my stance, even though she had already shown me that. When I employed that new technique it allowed me to meet the requirements. I like the new model better than the irritated old one."

Jack thanked the young man for his insight and made a mental note to cancel his need to talk to Su Li about her student's attitudes about her training.

CHAPTER SIXTEEN

Jack went to the work station in his apartment at 8 a.m. when he had a vision.

He was standing alone looking down on the RHONE building in Bern, Switzerland. He heard God tell him, *"This demon-ridden group has defied me for too long. They have ignored the warning you gave them. They say that not even God can stop them now. I want the Crossfire Team to totally destroy this temple to Satan and make it a definite statement that will make everyone know that I am Elohim. I will place my word into the hearts of the other men and leaders of the RHONE that I will not tolerate any more of their rebellion. Do this thing quickly. I will be with you as will my angels as you battle for My Kingdom."*

Jack snapped back to reality and took a deep breath. He now knew he needed to come up with a solution to the RHONE headquarters destruction immediately. He called Charlie Wu and asked him to come to the apartment for a meeting.

Charlie showed up in less than four minutes and sat down next to Jack in the Mini-War Room annex in Jack's apartment. "What can I do for you, Jack?"

Jack looked at the always upbeat but mostly unreadable man. "Charlie, I'm asking you instead of Ethan primarily because of your greater experience, especially in spy work. Can you weasel your way into the USAF Space Command and use one of those ceramic-encased kinetic weapons without their knowledge or at least so that they cannot trace it back to us?

Charlie thought about that for several minutes. "I think we could do that, once. After that they would close any loopholes I can use this time. What is the target?"

Jack grimaced, "The RHONE headquarters building in Bern, Switzerland. God told me to destroy it and the people there completely as quickly as we can."

Charlie shook his head. "I see why you'd want to use a needle from space rather than HARP. They are too close to the city and its citizens for an earthquake. But, there will still be some collateral damage from the destruction of the RHONE headquarters via space needle because it will be equivalent to a 20,000-pound directed munitions weapon and that will cause a whole lot of shaking to be goin' on."

Jack asked, "Is there any way we could minimize the collateral damage?"

Charlie thought about that. "Possibly, let me run some projections and I'll let you know in the next ten minutes."

Jack nodded and turned back to his planning.

Eight minutes later Charlie was back. "Okay, I think we have a solution to the majority of the collateral damage issue. I will have the needle come in at a twenty-degree angle over the downtown area which adds a vector to the destruction away from there. The entire headquarters building will be destroyed. A fortuitous by-product of the angling will be to drop the remains of the destroyed building into a massive crevasse in the upper part of the Earth's mantle that is just to the SSW of the building, according to the Land Sat data. You want me to do it?"

Jack said, "No, I don't want you to do it, I'm ordering you to do it. Any criminal or spiritual repercussions are on me, not you. Make it happen around eleven a.m. their time to wipe out the most staff you can. Let's see...Bern is one hour behind Tel Aviv time. Also, just before you release the needle for the strike is there a way to tap into a Land Sat and see infrared signatures of bodies in the building at the top levels?"

Charlie looked at his notes. "Best I could do is around 10:30 a.m. their time for a quick look-see. You want to see if the big boss is in his office for the big event?"

Jack grinned, "Yes, I do. I also want to make sure it's not a Swiss Holiday."

Charlie checked the time. "Okay, it's almost 10:00 a.m. there so I've got to take a look at the Land Sat information in thirty minutes. Then I have to make the needle drop from the third satellite in fifty-five minutes to have it hit the building precisely at 11:00 a.m."

Charlie stared at Jack for a minute. "You do realize that Marco Marino will make this action a terroristic attack on the RHONE. Not just a reprisal attack for all the attacks they have laid on us through their assassins?"

Jack nodded his head. "All I can tell you is that the Father of the Universe told me to totally destroy that building and the staff inside of the building. The OWG and Marco have turned everything around so that good is evil and evil is good. A better question to ask me is, "Do I care?" My answer is, "No, I don't care." The building houses the people who God says are, rebellious and demon-ridden. End of story. I know that in the current world political scene this makes us the criminals but I work for the Creator of the Universe."

Charlie smiled, "Ten-Four, boss, I will get it done. Video on line three in fifty minutes."

Jack sat in his room for thirty minutes and then went down to the War Room. He noticed that it was a full house. Most all of the Core Team and the SOG were sitting, standing, or walking around in the War Room. Word had gotten around about the strike against the RHONE. There was a momentary Land Sat view of the building in the Infrared scan mode. Hundreds of people could be seen sitting or walking in and through the building's ten stories. Jack looked at the area of the leader's office and saw about fifteen people attending a meeting there.

A countdown clock set of numerals appeared in white superimposed on the screen as the exterior of the building was shown again. There were only seventeen seconds left before the clock showed 00:00:00.

CHAPTER SEVENTEEN

The Supreme Leader of the RHONE, Marc Tronat looked out at the fourteen top level officers of the RHONE who were attending his meeting at the top of RHONE's Headquarters Base to hear the important news that only the Supreme Leader was privy to so far. They were the best of the best and would eventually be placed in control of a large part of the world as Regional Leaders. Tronat knew that the major stumbling block to their operations so far was the accursed Crossfire Team. Well, these men would be glad to know that he was about to terminate the entire team and end to their reign of irritation and blockage. Councilors had warned him that the Crossfire Team had the Jewish God on their side and it would be impossible to stop them.

Marc Tronat had silently laughed at their fantasies, He knew that their God wasn't real and he was about to prove it to the whole world. He reveled in the fact that other than Marco Marino, Marc Tronat was the most powerful man in the known universe. Now that he knew for certain where the retched team of troublemakers lived he would destroy their hidden Island Base and them with it!

At that selfsame Sea Base the countdown timer reached 00:00:00. The close up K11 Keyhole Satellite image of the RHONE building was crystal clear. In that clarity the entire Team watched as the building suddenly crumpled like a building of sand and dissolved into shattered debris and bodies. The entire ten-story building exploded and imploded at the same time. The ground below the building dissolved into fragments and particles and like the trapdoor below the hangman's noose all of the debris and chunks tumbled out of sight. The entire building and its four subterranean basements, its parking lots, and all of its walls and barricades simply disappeared from sight.

The ground continued to tremble and millions of tons of rocks including a large mountain foothill followed the fragments of building into a crevasse of giant proportions.

When the dust settled there remained a massive crater over a half-mile in diameter and 100 feet deep that displayed the top of one Billion tons of rock.

Emergency crews from Bern pulled to a stop on the road that used to lead to the entire RHONE site and turned off their lights. There wasn't anything anyone could do and there wasn't anything left to do it to either.

Jack flipped the controls to a Prime News station and watched the ground level videos of the first News responders to the "disaster" outside of Bern. It was almost like a non-event as there was no burning building or even a collapsed building to use as a backdrop to the talking heads that were bemoaning the loss to the Nation of Switzerland, in payroll if for no other reason.

Jack led a prayer for the souls of any that had perished that knew the Lord and then dismissed the troops.

Charlie walked into the War Room that now only held Jack and Laura. "Jack, you may be in charge but I pushed the button that terminated all those lives. I prayed and asked God to forgive me and learned that I had nothing to be forgiven for. God told me that He authorized the destruction and there was no guilt in doing what he tells us to do."

Jack nodded. "Do you think the story will come out about "how" this happened? Will Marino make the Air Force come clean about losing one of their Space Needles?"

"No, this is still a classified and Ultra-Top Secret project that the world doesn't know about. I don't think they'll say anything about losing control of one of their Top Secret inertia weapons. That needle was moving at hypersonic speeds and I doubt that anyone out there will have seen, or recorded, anything about the method of destruction with the exception of ourselves

Jack's phone rang and he answered it. "Yes, Director, Yes Ma'am, that was our response to their multiple attempts at killing us individually and corporately. No, I didn't know that, and thank you for letting me know that. Yes, Ma'am, No Ma'am. Yes, Ma'am we will talk about this later. Goodbye Director."

Jack hung up and sat there bemused. He looked up at the other two people. "It seems that we were not the only ones to be watching the destruction of the RHONE building.

It seems that the Mossad tracked the needle from its platform and predicted where it would hit. The Director was interested in our participation in that event. I told her it was our effort to repay the RHONE for all their attacks on us. Then she told me that they had just found out that a traitor in their group had leaked the location of the Crossfire Team to the RHONE in exchange for a large amount of money.

The Mossad attempted to arrest the traitor who tried to fight his way out of his predicament and died in the effort. It also seems that the RHONE was about to pay an even larger sum to a Chinese dissident to use China's HARP capability to destroy the island that the flight tunnel is in. That dissident also died in an escape attempt this morning. According to the Mossad's information the dissident had no knowledge of what the target meant to anyone and even if he did he took that information to the grave."

Jack looked at Laura. "I congratulated her as to the successful conclusion to both of our efforts and told her that we would see her in the near future concerning our efforts. Charlie, I think I want you there also."

Charlie smiled, "Of course, General."

CHAPTER EIGHTEEN

The most immediate sign they had really hurt the RHONE was that there were no more assassins to be found in or around Tel Aviv. Many of the known assassins had quickly left Israel right after the destruction of the RHONE headquarters building.

Over the next two weeks more signs and hints started appearing around the world indicating that the RHONE had started to self-destruct. Soldiers were defecting and living to tell about it. That greatly emboldened thousands more to follow suit. The leaders tried to consolidate their commands but there was no one over them or anyone to give them pay or supplies. Many leaders either tried to confiscate everything they could out of selfishness or disappeared themselves. The ever present demonic influence evaporated and with it went the complete command structure and the SS division.

In the larger divisions many of the troops broke out as a group and set themselves up as Mercenaries. They started shopping for customers they could work for with some degree of control and comfort. Several groups were approached to find, attack, or eliminate the Crossfire Team. To a man they declined those offers. They had seen or heard about indestructible soldiers and golden and silver warriors that wore armor that deflected bullets and bomb blasts. They did not want to lose their first encounters as independent Mercenaries.

For the next two weeks' life settled down at the Sea Base and the training schedule was relaxed somewhat. All of the Core Team training managers were kept busy bringing new members up to speed.

Jack's class was treated to a refresher class with the angel Hugo in sword techniques.

Jack decided to use the break in the training classes he had holding. He found Laura, "Honey, I am going to see Rabbi Chanan about a resident Rabbi for the Sea Base Synagogue. I arranged a meeting at the Rabbi's Synagogue for noon today."

Laura looked thoughtful for a few seconds. "I think I would like to go with you, if that is alright."

Jack smiled, "It's alright with me and probably will be for the Rabbi. I'm not sure of any restrictions that Jewish Synagogues have about women so let's be flexible if he has concerns."

Laura nodded. She went to get cleaned up after her Martial Arts class.

Since the assassins had abandoned their efforts to eliminate the Crossfire Team when the RHONE collapsed, Jack wasn't too worried about him and Laura being attacked on the way to the Synagogue and back.

The Rabbi met them warmly at the front door of the Synagogue. "Mr. and Mrs. Malone, it is a pleasure meeting with you both again. I have often wondered how you all were doing in your unique line of work. General Levy and I speak of you and your team frequently."

Jack smiled, "It is our pleasure to meet with you again Rabbi. We all would like to thank you for your support of our operations with the leaders of Israel."

The Rabbi smiled back. "They can be a volatile group sometimes but I am reassured by your survival that you are still keeping Israel safe from demons. For that we all thank you."

They discussed the course of activities since they fateful meeting at the portal to the Sea Base six months ago. Jack brought the Rabbi up to date and then presented his request for a Rabbi to serve as a spiritual leader at the Sea Base. Jack continued, "We would, of course, open up the Synagogue to all Jewish personnel at the Sea Base. That would include all of the Mossad personnel on the other side of the base as well as all the members of the Team."

The Rabbi thought for a few seconds. The he asked, "Would the Rabbi be subjected to demonic events like the one we experienced?"

Jack shook his head. "If he remains in the Sea Base I doubt that he will meet any demons because the Angels of God guard the Sea Base and that precludes any attempts by Satan to get his followers into the base proper."

Rabbi Chanan nodded his head. "Then I think I know just the man for the job. His name is Rabbi Joshua Epstein and he is an excellent Rabbi. He is the son of Rabbi Hiram and Sarah Epstein of Jerusalem and has a tremendous knowledge of Torah and Rabbinical teachings. He is forward thinking and very modern for a Rabbi. I expect great things from him. Your posting would be an excellent foundation and challenge for him."

Rabbi Chanan nodded his head. "I and my council will pray about this. If G-d is willing, I will contact young Epstein and see if he is willing to assume your Synagogue. If all the answers are *yes*, then I will bring him and we will meet at your base and discuss the position. You see, you have to approve of him and he has to approve of you."

The Rabbi stared at the young couple for several minutes and then made a startling announcement. "I see that G-d has anointed both of you as the Priest of your team. This is a good step you are taking. I expect great things of this union between Judeo-Christians and Jews."

Jack and Laura thanked the Rabbi and left for the Sea Base with a good feeling about their new Rabbi.

CHAPTER NINETEEN

Later that afternoon Laura got a call from Elon requesting her presence at the Mossad side of the Sea Base. She thought about the last meeting she had with Elon and dressed accordingly. Then she knelt and prayed to God and asked Him if this was a wise thing to do and for protection. She felt the grace and peace of the Creator of the Universe fall down over her and she sang her song of worship and love to Him. She sensed a presence and looked up expecting to see the angel Rose.

To her surprise she saw her Savior standing before her. She wanted to bow with her head to the floor but He reached out and lifted her to her feet. She heard in her mind his sweet voice. *"Laura, it is right for you to go on this mission as requested by Elon. He needs to mature in the spirit and part of that maturing will be his learning respect for you as you teach him. This problem is only a very small part of a much bigger problem which this will expose. The Father does not want this larger problem to continue. I am sending you as my hand to prevent a major event from occurring. Go, and I will be with you. Stand firm in your faith and your love for Me and the Father."*

Yahshua was gone and Laura knelt down and prayed her thankfulness to both Yahveh and Yahshua. Getting to her feet she reached up and carefully keyed the hidden microphone as part of her combat communications gear. Jack answered quickly.

Laura explained Elon's call and the Master's commands. Then she grinned. "I'm going over to the Mossad side of the base now. Keep a watch over me and pray for my ability to do Yahshua's work."

While she had been explaining things Jack had been praying and his spirit agreed with her and her decision. "Don't worry about that my love. I too, will not be too far away."

As Laura started her short trip Jack filled Mark and Sarah in on the event. "Mark, Sarah, I have to present our case against the RHONE to General Levy in two hours.

Guard my wife for me and keep me updated. I know with you two around she couldn't be in better hands. We're both counting on your best efforts. If possible, please try not to tick off the Mossad or render too many of them useless. Capiche?"

Mark smiled, "Not to worry buddy, we've got this!" As Jack disconnected the call he also smiled. His random thought was that the Mossad had better walk softly around Laura because by herself she was a force to be reckoned with. With the Connellys included it could be a game changer for anyone involved. He relaxed and went back to his presentation for the head of the IDF.

Laura looked good dressed in her BDUs and Ray Ban sunglasses. Her blonde hair was combed back and up under her BDU hat and she felt "good".

She drove one of the travel carts over to the Mossad side of the Sea Base and got off near their main entrance. Walking over to the receptionist manning a small booth in front of the entrance she asked to see Elon and explained that he had asked her to make the trip over from the Crossfire Team side of the base.

The man got up and exited the booth and extended his hand. "Glad to meet you Mrs. Malone. I saw you as you arrived and have already told Elon you were here. I have to ask you to leave your sidearm with me." This was presented in a dignified manner and not as a demand. Laura complied and gave her 40 caliber XD automatic to the guard. He placed it in a lock box and gave her a badge with her name on it and a list of clearances listed on one side.

Elon exited the front door and greeted her cordially.

"Laura, thank you for coming. The Mossad has run into a situation that requires a better understanding of Christianity than I yet possess. I suggested they read you into the situation and see if you are interested in getting involved." They walked into the Mossad part of the base and down a short hall. She was interested in how their neighbors had set up their base compared to the Crossfire Team side.

Elon keyed an elevator and they traveled several floors down. The door opened and Laura could of sworn that they were at the Mossad Headquarters building in Tel Aviv. Everything looked quite similar.

Elon showed her to an office and gave her a seat. He also sat on her side of the desk. Less than a minute went by before another man walked into the office and closed the door before welcoming Laura to their base. He smiled, "Mrs. Malone, my name is Ephraim Tallon. I am in charge of the operations run out of our base here. He took the command position behind the desk and picked up a folder. He opened it and then sat back in his chair. He looked up at Laura. "I asked Elon to invite you here today so that we could discuss a sticky situation with small group of Christian women about ten blocks away from the Portal in Tel Aviv. I asked Elon to accompany you here as a liaison. I know he now works for the Crossfire Team and yet, he has many good connections with the Kidon here and is highly respected by the operating personnel."

Laura nodded to Ephraim, "Please tell me what the problem is and I will see if I can assist you."

Ephraim seemed somewhat embarrassed to discuss the problem but plowed on regardless. "Information was given to us concerning a local Hezbollah terrorist we are actively seeking. The information indicated that one or more of the women in a group home is supplying and housing this terrorist. His name is Farok Abdullah."

The Mossad leader withdrew a photo from the folder on the desk and showed it to Laura. It showed a young Arab man with intense brown eyes with a rag mop hairstyle. The stern, hardened look on his face made him look driven, or hunted. She made sure the picture was captured by the video camera on her body armor.

Ephraim shook his head. "Our normal procedure would be to interrogate all of the women there and if there was an indication of complicity we would arrest everyone involved. But, this group is complaining to their Judeo-Christian Synagogue that we are harassing them because they are Christians. I asked Elon to discuss the situation with them but they rejected his approach because one of the women knew him when he was part of the Kidon and very Jewish. He suggested that you could possibly talk to them as one Christian to another and either set their minds at ease concerning our intentions or discern whether or not any, or all, of them are involved with Farok."

Laura smiled, "Thank you for the vote of confidence but wouldn't their Rabbi be more effective in soliciting their cooperation?"

Elon spoke up, "Yes, but he doesn't have any combat experience and believes the best of everyone. Very noble, but he is not a detective who's been in the thick of battle and can weight one in the balance of good and evil."

Laura smiled, "Okay, where do I find these damsels in distress?"

Ephraim tipped his head toward Elon. "I believe Elon can steer you in the right direction. Just talk to them and see if you can get a feeling about their allegiance to Farok or to Israel."

Elon and Laura left the Mossad half of the base. Laura retrieved her handgun and checked the load and holstered it. They checked out with the Mossad personnel and walked out of the main Portal. Eight blocks later Elon pointed out one of the apartment buildings and told her, Ms. Brighton's apartment is number 34 on the third floor. I believe that there are six women living there. Ms. Brighton is Ephraim's suspect for collaboration with Farok. Shall I stay close?"

Laura looked at Elon as she inquired of the Lord. She shook her head. "No, I am sure that if they see you they will know the Mossad is involved in my being here. I'll call you if I need you. Thank you for recommending me."

Elon smiled and turned and headed back to the Sea Base.

Laura prayed and asked God if what she was doing was what He wanted her to do and asked for wisdom as to a good reason for visiting this stranger.

She leaned back against a sun baked wall with her eyes closed as she thought about an acceptable purpose for her call. A thought formed that definitely wasn't her own. She nodded and opened her eyes. Fixing everything on the street in her mind she walked across the street and up the six steps to the locked front door. She rang the bell button for Apartment 34 and waited.

CHAPTER TWENTY

The door next to her buzzed and she pushed it open. There was no elevator so Laura walked up the three flights of stairs to the proper floor and walked down the hall to the right apartment. She knocked on the door and a twenties to thirties year old woman opened the door. The two women sized each other up. The woman at the door asked, in English, "Yes, what can I do for you?"

Laura smiled, "Hi, my name is Laura and I represent a Christian organization that investigates cases of harassment by the Jews on Christians. I was given this address and the name, Ms. Brighton, as a possible case of harassment by the Mossad. I wanted to determine if there is anything my organization can do to help her."

Short, to the point, and simple.

The woman at the door blinked several times and then asked, "What is the name of your organization?"

Laura smiled again, "The Crossfire Team". We tend to avoid publicity and work in the background. Most of the time you would only hear about us in court or on the streets."

The woman nodded, "Okay, please come in, Laura."

They walked into the living room space and sat down in two overstuffed chairs facing each other. The woman stuck her hand out, "I am Rita Brighton and I am concerned about an investigation the Jewish Mossad is prosecuting against one of the women that live in this apartment."

Laura thought for a second. Ephraim and Elon had indicated that Rita was the suspect. She took a small pad of paper out of her side pocket and a pen and jotted down the details.

"What is the woman's name they are investigating and what is the Mossad investigating her for?"

Rita rolled her eyes, "Her name is Sheila Yabaran and the detectives questioned her, three different times, about a man she dated two months ago. It is so ridiculous!"

Laura asked who the man was and what the "detectives" wanted to know about her relationship with this man.

Rita sighed, "Apparently they believe that this man, his name is Farok, something, is a terrorist. He is an Arab but he's no terrorist. Sheila said that he was a nice young man and is interested in science and the arts."

Laura thought for a few seconds. "Rita, did you ever meet this Farok?"

Rita nodded her head. "Once, when he came to pick up Sheila. He seemed nice to me."

Laura nodded her head in sympathy. "Usually, when the Mossad is interested in someone they will watch that person and where they live. Have they placed men, and sometimes, women, near your apartment building or following Sheila?"

Rita held her hands up in a gesture of innocence, "I don't know if they have or not but they keep coming back. They've been here three times already and they subtly promised there would be more "meetings" until they find Farok or determine that he is not a possible terrorist. Do you think your group can help get them off or our backs?"

Laura tipped her head to one side. "I'm not sure yet. Do you or Sheila have any idea where this Farok person is? Or, has he reconnected with Sheila? This would be a chance to talk to him and see if he can clear this up. It's probably a case of mistaken identity. Clear that up and the Mossad has to leave you alone."

Rita shook her head. "I haven't seen him in several months and I don't think Sheila has either. She said that she wished she'd never gone out with him because this is so upsetting to all of us."

Laura asked "When could I talk to Sheila?"

Rita looked at her watch. "She'll be off work in about two hours."

Laura started to get up and then seemed to think of another question. "Where does Sheila work?"

Rita blinked again, "Why?"

Laura smiled, "Just in case this Farok has tried to see her somewhere other than here. I might get a chance to speak with him there."

Rita thought for a few seconds. "Sheila works as a planning specialist for the IDF here in Tel Aviv. You can talk to her about that when you come back to see her."

Laura thanked Rita for her cooperation and told her that she would be in touch later today. Rita let her out of the apartment and closed the door behind her.

Laura left the building and walked to and through several stores in the event someone was following her. She made her way back to the Portal and Ephraim's office.

Ephraim looked at her expectantly. Laura took out her notebook and summed things up. "Rita Brighton is lying if your claim is true that she is Farok's friend. Rita indicated that Farok had dated a Sheila Yabaran one time and that neither Sheila nor she herself has had any contact with Farok since that time, several months ago. I am also concerned that "Sheila's" job is as a planning specialist for the IDF here in Tel Aviv. The other thing that raised a red flag is that even though Rita twice mentioned that she felt that the Mossad was harassing her, and Sheila yet failed to ask for assistance or legal advice to help with a case of harassment."

Ephraim opened the folder on his desk and read it for a minute. "Well, your suspicions are well founded. Rita Brighton is the woman involved with Farok." He took a series of small pictures out of the folder and showed them to Laura. Obviously shot with a long lens, a high-speed camera, and fast emulsion film. There were eight pictures of Rita and Farok together, talking, and kissing.

Ephraim sighed, "She also lied to you about the job at the IDF. She is the one working there. And, it was a manager at the IDF that alerted us to Farok because she tried to get him into her office twice but the security would not allow it."

Laura grinned, "Based on several past events I am well aware of the Mossad's ability to "interrogate" a prisoner and produce sufficient and usually damning information. Why don't you simply arrest her and "ask" her the hard questions?"

"Because of politics, that's why. Rita is the daughter of Hiram Brighton who is one of the Likud party leading lights. Likud believes in maintaining the status quo. Thus, Likud supports legislative and other arrangements designed to insure the authority of the Orthodox Rabbinate in all matters of personal status and religious practice in Israel. If we were to arrest his daughter on suspicions only and "sweated" her with no results he would campaign across Israel for the complete elimination of the Mossad and everyone in it. I know, not a good reason in the light of national security. But, here in Israel it is a fact of life. My boss says not to touch her without proof of her complicity in something serious. Our hands are tied until we have some proof."

Laura nodded her head. "That's not too dissimilar from American politics these days. I have a chance to talk to Sheila later this afternoon. Considering the multiple lies Rita has already given to me, I would suspect that the second meeting would be a trap for me. But, I understand your conundrum and will hold that second meeting. You, the Mossad, and the Kidon have worked hard and taken terrible risks and losses to aid us in our missions. I would like the chance to return the favor."

Elon looked somewhat stricken. "Laura, I cannot, in good consciousness let you walk in there alone. I will be shadowing you and if anything is amiss I will be there for you."

Laura smiled at Elon's gallantry. "Thanks Elon, you might have to stand in line. Remember, we work as a team? She spoke into the air, "Right guys?" Laura turned on her speaker mode.

Sarah spoke back to Laura. "Right!"

Ephraim frowned, "How can you get communications in and out of this building?"

Ephraim's cell phone rang and he answered it. He was staring at a live picture of Sarah Connelly. "Hello Ephraim, you would be surprised how easy it is to penetrate your security. But, we are your friends so that should not be a problem." The picture faded out.

Elon smiled, "Oh, I see, okay."

Laura walked out of Ephraim's office and found a bench in the hall. She sat down and prayed.

CHAPTER TWENTY-ONE

Mark called Ethan Reaper in the control room of the COMM/SEC (Communications/Security) Department and asked Ethan to lock onto Laura's ID necklace and track her. He also asked Ethan to keep an electronic eye on her and her environment.

As Laura walked up the front steps to Rita Brighton's apartment house she glanced up and down the street. She noticed both Mark and Sarah in an SUV two doors down from the building. She keyed her combat microphone and said, "Thanks guys". She heard two clicks called Squelch Tails in her earpiece.

She rang apartment 34 and the door buzzed. Entering the door, she used a folded piece of cardboard as a small shim and placed it at the hinge side of the door which would keep the door from locking shut.

She heard a command tone in her right ear as Ethan contacted her and her team. "Laura, be aware that there are three people in the third floor apartment numbered 34. Two of them have readings of handguns."

Laura clicked her microphone twice to confirm her receipt of the message. She reached the third floor and walked to the door. She knocked on the door and Rita opened the door. Laura asked if Sheila was home.

Rita smiled, "Yes, she is, come on in."

Laura walked into the apartment with her nerves wired tight. She went to the living room and stood there while Rita went to get Sheila.

Rita walked back in with another woman that Laura assumed was Sheila. Laura introduced herself and explained what her organization attempted to do for people that felt they were being harassed by Israeli Authorities such as the Mossad. Sheila nodded her head and suggested that they move back into her work area and discuss the problems. Laura heard Ethan's voice again in her right ear. "The third person is moving toward you on your left."

Laura rotated somewhat to her left and smiled at the two women. Just then, her spirit reacted to a definite demonic force. Laura purposely hesitated before she prayed to keep her armor and sword unrevealed.

As Sheila stepped out of the room, a second door opened and an armed man stepped into the living room.

Laura looked the man and his gun over. "You would be Farok, I assume."

Farok nodded his head and gestured with his pistol for Laura to walk in front of him into the next room. Just then Ethan said loudly into to her right ear. "I've got signs of demonic activity right there!"

Laura had reached the point that she had been waiting for and started to pray in her prayer language. The golden armor and the sword of the word blasted into sight and the esteem of Yahveh poured off of the blade of the sword. Both women screamed and Farok changed into a sleek black demon with a slim black blade.

Laura stepped forward and acted as if she was going to do a cross-body slash from her right to her left which caused the demon to swing its blade into a left vertical block. Instead, Laura spun around on the ball of her left foot and beheaded the demon which suddenly had no way to block that attack. Laura kept moving quickly and placed her sword right at Rita's neck as "Farok" the demon dissolved into slime and smoke.

There was a crash behind Laura as the door to the apartment was violently kicked out of its frame and Mark and Sarah rushed into the room. They were followed by less than two steps by Elon. All three people were armed and were wearing full body armor and helmets with visors.

Laura's armor was still active as she quietly told Rita that she was under arrest for demonic as well as terroristic charges. The woman's eyes were wide open and Laura could see panic in them.

Laura didn't do anything but harden her tone of her voice. "Tell me what Farok was doing and planning, NOW!"

Rita didn't dare to swallow in fear of slicing her throat on Laura's blade. She said, "I really don't know anything he, it, told me to help it find records at my job. But! I couldn't get it in there and it didn't tell me which files."

Mark had moved up to the woman. "Farok had to give you something that will narrow down what he was looking for. Think about what he said."

Laura stopped praying in her mind and the armor and the sword disappeared as she stepped back from Rita. That really didn't mean anything because Mark was right there with his assault rifle pointed generally in the vicinity of Rita's chest.

Rita let out a big breath that she had been holding while Laura's sword was at her throat. "He said that he wanted to understand the layout of the IDF command building. I couldn't give him much because I was never allowed out of my section." She looked with fear at Elon who was moving behind her and fastening manacles to her wrists.

Elon stared at her for a few seconds and then said, "Your father is going to be very disappointed in his little girl."

Rita looked down and nodded her head.

As Elon led Rita out the door Mark told him that he would have Ethan send her father a record of the discussion they had just had with his daughter and her confessions.

Laura didn't leave the apartment and Sarah picked up on her uneasiness. "What's the problem?"

Laura said, "There is unfinished business here. My direction from the Lord was. *This problem is only a very small part of a much bigger problem which this will expose. The Father does not want this larger problem to continue. I am sending you as my hand to prevent a major event from occurring.*"

CHAPTER TWENTY-TWO

Elon stepped over the smashed door and entered the apartment after turning the suspect over to a Mossad quick response team. He walked over to the foursome in the living room.

Mark was looking at Laura with concern. "What do you mean? This was just the beginning of a major problem?"

Laura started to nod her head when she had a major catch in her spirit. She started to pray and her armor and sword suddenly appeared. Startled, Mark and Sarah also started to pray and their armor appeared. Laura looked at Elon, "Pray! Now!" Elon started to pray and for the first time he was covered in silver armor and his sword appeared in his hand. He was so startled that he stopped praying and the armor faded out. Laura sternly said. "Keep praying, constantly!"

Elon realized his error and started praying again. His armor and sword reappeared.

Laura turned toward the front door and went to high guard with her sword. The other three spread out and also went to high guard position. Mark spoke into his combat microphone and told Ethan to get a reserve swords team to their address immediately.

With multiple cracking's and creaking's three different rifts appeared in the dimensional wall equally around the four warriors. Suddenly two dozen of the middle level demons exited the rifts and surrounded the four warriors but kept their swords lowered.

Laura was praying furiously for protection and guidance for all four of the warriors when she heard, *"Lower your swords and go with these demons. Do not talk to them and stay on your guard. You cannot defeat them yet."*

The demons in the rift ahead of the Team moved to their right and held their left hands out to indicate that the Team members should willingly go into the rift ahead of them. Mark frowned, "I think this could be a really, really bad move."

Laura shook her head. "Yahshua said to do it." She walked ahead of the others and walked into the rift. Sarah would not abandon her friend and followed her. Neither of the men would let anything happen to the two women and so they followed Sarah. The demons walked into the rift and all three rifts closed with a bang!"

Mark moved up to walk next to Laura and said, "I really think this was a bad move. The owner of this realm is extremely unhappy with all of us, but, especially with me. Please tell me that you are sure it was Yahshua that told you to do this."

Laura said, "Yes, it was Yahshua and he wants us to stop some major demonic doing so get a grip and remember who our God is."

Mark grinned, "Ouch, that hurt."

Sarah was listening to the talk and added, "Your unbelief was showing a little bit there my love."

Elon asked, "Where are we?"

Sarah laughed, "It would have been more correct to ask, "Where in the hell are we?" remember to keep praying."

The light ran to the red spectrum and it was fairly dim while they walked. Elon looked back and then faced forward again. "Our escort is right behind us but don't look as aggressive as normal."

The tunnel they were walking through opened out into a large cavern and there were hundreds of demons doing unexplainable things all over the place.

A large red demon appeared ahead of the Team Members and they came to a halt directly in front of it. The demon said, "Our Master has asked that we bring you here so that he can speak to you."

No one spoke back. The demon vanished and Laura said urgently, "Pray for a covering in the blood of Yahshua now. Satan will attempt to curse you while he is talking to you. Ask Yahveh to block all assignments and curses and return them to the sender."

A few seconds later with a little showmanship of lightning and thunder, Satan appeared in front of the quartet. Satan held up his right hand and all noise stopped and all the other demons stopped moving. Satan stared at the four humans with a contemptuous sneer on his face.

"Your lives hang on my whim. Do not attempt to negotiate or deal with me. I am all powerful here! I...I will tell you what is to happen. You will do as I say or you will die."

Laura noted that the devil was somewhat put off or rattled and it was interfering with his speech. Probably it was his inability to place curses or assignments on them.

Mark made the comment to Elon, "He always tries to talk us to death before he gets around to the point."

Actual flames came out of the devil's nose and ears. "Mark Connelly, we have unfinished business that will be finalized soon."

Mark nodded his head and stared at the devil with an "I can't wait to humble you again" look on his face.

Sarah was concerned that Mark would actually make the devil go insane and that would not be good.

It actually took the devil several minutes to regain his composure. He then thundered his demand. "You four will carry a message to the leaders of Israel for me. If you will do that, I will let you live this time."

Satan studied the four people in their glowing armor and swords with the esteem of Yahveh by their sides. He could not detect any fear in any of them. He knew it was God isolating them from the curses of fear and helplessness that he was directing against them.

"Tell the leaders of Israel that I, Satan, have seen the future and they will kneel to Marco Marino and give him total control of Jerusalem or they will die at my bidding!"

He was fuming inside because they were as impervious to his anger as they were his curses. He laughed to show his superiority. He told them "Leave while you can. "Next time I will settle matters between us."

The devil stared at them as they didn't move. The anger in him rose to new heights and he so wanted to destroy them with his own hands. But, he felt the sight of the God of the Universe on him. He said, "All demons leave my sight, NOW!"

When there were no demons to be seen, Satan knelt to one knee and mumbled something. None of the four warriors moved or said a word. Satan, at this point, was glaring daggers that were real and they smashed the walls of the cavern but didn't bother the four humans.

Finally, he said in an audible voice, "Mark Connelly, I apologize for illegally trapping you in Jerusalem and attempting to kill you." He stared death at the four, but especially Mark. "Now leave before I forget my agreements and tear you all limb from limb!

Laura turned around and started walking back along the path they had taken to get there. Sarah, Elon, and Mark trooped along behind her. They seemed to walk for an exceptionally long time until a rift was opened before them and they stepped back into the human dimension. The rift snapped shut behind them and their armor and swords faded from view.

The four of them looked around in the dark. They were inside of some kind of building with a lot of concrete. Mark said, "Well, he let us go, but where are we?"

Sarah said, "This is the human dimension and we are on Earth. But, what do you think the devil did with us?"

Laura tried their communications without success. "I don't have any idea but I do know that we are not dressed for success in most cultures."

All four of them looked at each other in the dimness. Three of them had full body armor and M-8 carbines with grenade launchers.

Mark turned on the mapping feature of his comm gear and studied the inertial map that came up. He looked up and suggested that they find concealment quickly. He pointed to the west and all four of them loped along a dimly lit corridor until they found a small, empty room off of the corridor and went in and closed the door behind them. They sat down on the floor and Laura looked at Mark. "Okay, where in the devil are we?"

Mark shook his head. "According to my map we are smack dab in the middle of the most closely guarded area in all of North America other than the White House. We are in one of the most sensitive areas of Peterson Air Force Base. That means we have invaded the North American Aerospace Defense Command or NORAD, inside Cheyenne Mountain in Colorado Springs, Colorado. Other than putting us in a missile silo in a Soviet Missile complex he couldn't have found a better place than this to endanger our lives. My guess is that we will be caught, arrested and on our way to be buried in a terrorist prison somewhere in the next hour."

Laura said, "Why don't we pray and see what God has in mind for us to do."

Laura led the prayer and halfway through the prayer the door flew open to the room they were in and the lights came on in the room. There were four Military Police and several unarmed personnel who entered the room.

Nobody moved or said anything; because there really wasn't anything they could say and back up with proof.

The MPs looked around the room and the Sergeant leading the group shook his head. "Another dead end! I'm telling you that the security system has been hacked or its acting crazy. It identified this room as having multiple people in it. As you can see, it's empty." The personnel walked out ahead of the MPs who turned off the lights and shut and locked the door.

Laura laughed quietly. "I know what is going on. I really do. Satan put us here to mess us up as badly as possible without doing anything himself. God has neutralized that illegal advantage by making us "not here" and deleting the devil's edge. Now, how do we get back to Israel without the U.S. Government arresting the three of us and Elon just because he's with us?"

CHAPTER TWENTY-THREE

The four people continued to pray and Sarah got a word. She smiled, "It is fairly simple. We walk out of the base and find an area away from the site. Then we use our cell phones to call the Sea Base and request a ride home on the "Ghost".

Mark shook his head, "This isn't like walking out of an elementary school. There are barriers that have to be moved so we can leave. We have to have the correct badges and documentation to even get to the place where we can leave the base. So, I suggest we get started."

It turned out to be just as simple as Sarah said. They walked through the base and no one saw them. No cameras detected them and when they reached the large blast doors to the outside world they just had to wait twenty minutes until an approved truck left the base and then they walked out with it.

Eventually they were completely away from the base and walking down an access road that led to the town of Colorado Springs when Mark had them walk a few hundred feet into a vacant field full of untended grass.

He took out his cell phone and called the Sea Base. He got one of the on-duty personnel in the COMM/SEC group. He had them connect him to Jack Malone.

Jack was jubilant when he heard from Mark. Mark gave him the cliff notes version of their recent activities. Jack had him wait while he contacted the Research group on the Sea Base Airfield and requested a special trip in the Ghost.

Fortunately, even though the Ghost was being modified and wouldn't be ready for the next two weeks, the Ghost II was available and after some discussion with the director of that group they made a plan. Jack got back on the phone with Mark. "They are sending the Ghost II and I'm going to be on it. Now their decision is that you four need to get to a point fifty miles to the east of Colorado Springs so that the advanced radars at the Cheyenne Mountain won't detect the Ghost II. Can you do that?"

Mark laughed, "How much time do we have before you're here?"

Jack computed the times and said, "Four hours give or take fifteen minutes."

Mark smiled, "We'll make it happen and you can home on my medallion. Here, someone wants to talk to you." He handed the phone to Laura and walked away so she could talk to her husband by herself.

Sarah asked him while Laura talked on the phone, "If no one can see us, how are we going to get fifty miles away from here in less than four hours?"

Mark shrugged, "I haven't forgotten how to hot wire a car."

Laura came over and handed the phone to Mark. "Thanks. He still loves me."

Elon asked, "I'm confused, did we accomplish our mission for the Savior or didn't we?"

Laura shook her head, "No we didn't and we still don't even know what the great evil is that we are supposed to stop. What was this all about? Was it an obedience run to see if we would go back to hell, in your case, or what?"

Mark smiled, "I think it was an obedience run for Satan, that's what I think it was."

Sarah tapped Mark on the shoulder. "Come on you juvenile delinquent, we've got to find a car for you to hot wire."

Three hours later the four people had distanced themselves from the purloined vehicle and waited for their ride.

Elon saw the Ghost II before any of the others. He pointed across several fields as the plane rapidly approached them and then it landed vertically.

After everyone was on board the plane took itself out of Colorado and eventually back to Israel and the Sea Base. This time there was no drama.

Laura went back to praying to see if she could determine what it was they were to stop for God. She got an urge to go to the living area of the Crossfire side of the Sea Base. Arriving she found sixteen people there waiting for her.

She sidled up next to Jack and asked what the meeting was about.

Jack smiled, "I don't know. God brought all of us together and then we waited for you. I thought you would know."

She nodded and stepped up to address the people there. "I suspect that God wants us all here to announce the "great evil" we are to stop. Let's get the ball rolling. Let's pray."

CHAPTER TWENTY-FOUR

As the group sang songs of praise to Yahveh and Yahshua the weight of the Spirit fell on everyone and then they began to worship, most in their prayer languages.

The song they were singing in honor of Yahshua took on a deeper sound and became clearer and stronger which enraptured everyone there. The singing took on a heavenly sound that was sweet and pure.

Jack opened his eyes to see a host of angels singing with the Team members. The song came to an end and the angels faded from view but the harmony of the song continued quietly. Jack saw the angel Rose dancing as she floated above the floor. She came to a halt in front of the assembled group and opened her eyes. Jack had never seen the beautiful face that Rose displayed this time. It was enough to bring tears of joy to his eyes.

Rose started to speak. "Warriors of Yahveh know that your beautiful praise and worship has ascended to the third heaven and I have been honored to bring you the Most High's word to answer your prayers."

Everyone watched Rose with full attention. "The Most High has watched all of you as you have grown in your faith and your service to Him. He knows that you are ready for your next major battle. Now hear the word of the God of the Universe." *"Warriors of the Crossfire Team, it saddens my heart to have to tell you that the warriors you have fought alongside with before have become an unwilling enemy to you. Marco Marino has demanded the government of the United States of America use their military forces, especially their special forces, to find and eliminate your team. Many of the soldiers are sorely tried in this matter but, are honor-bound to follow their Commander-in-Chief's orders. As of two days ago, the full might of the American Military has begun to search for you with the intent to kill all of you and destroy any bases you have. They are close to determining where the Sea Base is located. Once they are sure of that location they will attempt to attack it in every way possible. My children, I command you to use compassion in your efforts to prevent your destruction against such a powerful foe. Respond as you can, using all of your abilities, means, and efforts to prevent your destruction and an all-out war between the west and Israel. I will be with you as you convince the west not to prosecute you."*

Rose looked at the members assembled with a stern face and then smiled, "Remember, it is Satan who is behind this campaign to eliminate you. Convince him that war with your team is ill advised and will cost him more than he is willing to pay. Mark Connelly, you understand what needs to be done and you are the only one to lead such an effort. First, change the mind of the U.S. leader. Then, take such a toll on Satan and his minions that he will know that he will lose far more than he will gain in a war with the Crossfire Team." She faded out of sight.

Mark stood up and stared thoughtfully at the other fifteen people in the room. "I have been given a great honor by our God. The chastisement of both the government of the United States and the ultimate evil in the universe to the extent that they will NOT want to fight against us ever again. I plan to fulfill God's expectations and I will use every asset and person that the Crossfire Team has at its disposal to accomplish these goals. I suggest each of you return to your areas and prepare for war."

Jack stood up and shook his head. "To give you some good news about our new challenges, remember it is the Holy Spirit of God that will fight with us against our enemies. Be of good spirit and pray for success."

Jack asked for some of the people to remain with them to brainstorm their options to accomplish their goals.

After the majority of the Team members had gone to prepare; Jack and the remaining members went to the War Room and took their places. Jack turned on the recorders and took a short roll call. "Laura, Mark, Sarah, David, Alexis, Charlie and Linda, Elon, Ethan, and I make ten."

Jack looked at Mark, "What do you have in mind?"

Mark nodded his head. "I believe I have a basic plan but I have to check one thing first. I'll be right back." He got up and left the room. Eight minutes later he was back and he was grinning.

"Based on three previous incidents I believe that we can do the will of God and do it in the next ten days." Mark sat back and smiled.

Jack sat there and stared at Mark, waiting quietly.

Mark looked at the other nine people in the room. "Okay, based on the demonic submarine action, the Israeli coast nuclear weapon action, and the RHONE battlefield event, ten Team members can bring the fear of God in the form of the Crossfire Team to the President of the United States of America and to Satan with impact.

Laura grinned; she knew Mark meant what he said. "Okay Mark, how do we do that?"

"We use a new aircraft. One related to the Ghost Aircraft to get to Washington D.C. undetected. Then, we will go see the President and his cabinet so we can discuss his backing off from having the U.S. Military attack us." Mark grinned again, "Depending on how well this works then we will use a similar strategy on Satan."

Jack sighed, "I assume that you have this all figured out so that we can live through it and make it home safely?"Mark nodded, "Absolutely, this plan is rock solid."

Laura stood up. "Let's pray for complete coverage by God's angels and the power of the Holy Spirit to keep our plans from our enemies' ears."

CHAPTER TWENTY-FIVE

After praying for divine coverage to block the demonic from knowing their plans the team broke into two groups to plan their assault on the government of the U.S. and on the government of Hell.

Jack, David, Sarah, and Laura presented every known response that the government and the alphabet agencies would try to use on them. Mark, Alexis, Elon, Charlie, Linda, and Ethan defined a strategy to handle those responses.

One of the concerns was that the government would use one of the two Presidential doubles rather than the real President in the Presidential Bunker where the Team wanted to talk to the man.

Laura listened to the situation and spoke up. "All we have to do is pray and ask the Father if the real President is the one in the Bunker."

The other two problems could be the lack of surprise and either being confined in one position or running out of air and being suffocated. The Team tried to come up with adequate solutions to each of these problems. Jack prayed about getting to present themselves to the President and his Cabinet so that they could conduct business before the Secret Service spirited them away. Jack realized they needed help and he asked the Father in the name of Yahshua how to overcome the situation. Jack was treated to a mental picture of the scientist that developed the Force Generators in the first place.

He called Dr. Clashire in Colorado and explained all three problems. Dr. Clashire thought about these challenges for a few minutes. "Jack, I think we might have a solution for your needs. Let me think about it some more and pray about it. I'll get back to you in a few hours."

The Team took into account that each of the problems could have solutions that could be adopted before their travel to the U.S. and continued to plan their strategy on that basis.

After lunch they went back to the planning. Around two p.m. in the afternoon the scientist called back. "Jack, I believe we have an excellent solution to all three problems."

Jack turned on the voice recorders and told him to go ahead with his concepts.

Dr. Clashire chuckled. "The solution to the ability to arrive secretly is actually a different design specification of the Force Generator's basic operating process. I had run into a situation during the early development phase and it had bothered me considerably. After I got to the working model stage, the model would disappear during operation. I would shut things down and then the field collapsed and there was the Generator model. I spent two weeks until I found a modification that kept the field stable in the visible light spectrum without creating other problems."

"Now then", the Doctor started speaking again. "I have revisited the "problem" and by adding a switch to the top of the Generator you can select "normal" operation or "special" operation. When you select "special" operation you become undetectable, or for all intents and purposes, visually invisible. It is simply another function of the Force Generator's operation that doesn't just stop the "attacking" photons. The field automatically passes them around the field so that they exit on the other side from where they impact the field. If you are standing between two groups of people, the people on either side see the other people. You don't exist as far as visual identification goes. You can use the "special" mode and walk into a guarded area until you get to where you want to be. Then switching your Generator to "normal" mode you can be seen. In either case you cannot be injured or killed because the Generator is on. But, remember, even though you are visually invisible if you run into something or someone you will impact that thing or person."

Jack laughed, "Doctor that is a tailor-made solution to our present problem."

Doctor Clashire laughed with Jack. "Yes it is. But, I am not the tailor. That would be Yahveh, the creator of the universe. I didn't realize I was disabling one of the features of the Generator by my efforts to resolve the disappearing Generator on the test bench."

Jack then asked, "How about the other two problems with movement and air?"

Doctor Clashire sighed. "We can solve the movement problem through the field also. Again, my vision wasn't great enough to realize that was solved by the original design. I worked hard to find ways to get around this "problem" also not knowing that it was actually part of the design."

"To prevent being held in one position you can use one of two methods of escape. Both are actually spiritual in performance. If you become stuck in a position and want to extradite yourself, you simply have to "will" your Force Generator to move in a certain direction. Yahveh's Holy Spirit will use the elemental forces of the universe to power the move. I'm talking about being buried in sand like Laura was when she fell four thousand feet from the helicopter over Jordan. If she had known what I now know, she could have willed herself to move sideward or upward and the Force Generator field will move that way as far as you want because God will take you there. The same method will work if you're buried under ten tons of rocks or in a thick steel box."

Jack laughed out loud. "That is fantastic! What is the second method of escape?"

Dr Clashire let out a big breath. "Number two is far more destructive and I would not recommend it in a friendly area. If your shield is on and you are prevented from moving in a direction by say, a wall, you can focus your mind rather than your will and "see" the obstacle in front of you removed. I tried that here to make sure it works. I'm afraid I am going to have to foot the bill for a new containment building. I "saw" the containment building as an obstacle in my mind. It is now a pile of dust and rubble. Thank Yahveh that nobody was in it at the time."

Jack shook his head. "You wanted a sturdier building anyway. Just get it built and I'll cover the costs. Now, how soon can we get some new Generators with the second switch on the top?"

Doctor Clashire laughed quietly again. "I can honestly tell you that God is orchestrating this operation. Get your best mechanical/electronic person and I'll tell them how to make the changes. The mounting hole in the Generator is already there but it is covered up by the plate above it. I have already sent, overnight freight, the new switches to you. Have your engineer call me and I'll talk them through the first change or two and then it will be easy."

Jack looked at Mark who was grinning. "Get Megan Cole and have her prepare to modify the Generators."

Back on the phone Jack asked, "Doctor, what about the air problem? Do we just will a move so that we can get air instead of being where we can't get it?"

The Doctor chuckled again. "No, actually the Father also designed the normal requirements for human operation within the field. Previously, I had three different people test it for up to three days and nights. The air was replenished, somehow. I really doubt that I have the ability to understand how God does that. But, the air after seventy-two hours was just as new as it was when we started the tests."

Jack said, "Doctor, you have just saved us a lot of time, worry and money. Consider your bonus for this mission doubled."

"I appreciate it Jack. I know I have more money than I could possibly spend during the rest of my lifetime, but, I am funding so many Jewish and Christian ministries and charities that I think the IRS is going to create a new category just for me. This new money will probably push them completely over the edge."

After Jack hung up, he saw Mark repeating a silent mantra and asked what he was doing.

Mark's eyes glittered, "Do you realize how much power I have with a Force Generator? I'm just repeating the words "Walk in humility and thank God, over and over. This is heady stuff! Considering we've already fallen over five miles and landed without damage. We've survived a two megaton nuclear explosion at ten feet, and now we can move the field by our will and destroy things simply by "seeing" them destroyed! I have got to be humble or this will build up my pride and make me sin knowing how powerful I am!"

Jack shook his head. "Just remember, none of this works without God. You are simply using one of His tools, and that only when and as he wants you to."

Mark thought about that. "You're right! I started to lose sight of my role as a servant and wanted to think of myself as all powerful, which is definitely not the case. Thank you."

The next day the package from Dr. Clashire arrived and after a quick phone call he talked Megan through the first modification to the Force Generators. She then quickly modified the other thirty-five units herself.

Jack asked the scientist if the aircraft they were going to fly to the U.S. in could be fitted with a Force Generator to keep it safe and invisible. Dr. Clashire asked the Holy Spirit in his mind if that would work. He told Jack to take one of the extra units and simply mount it to a part of the airframe or a bulkhead and activate it in the "special" mode. The size of the protected person or object wasn't an issue. If Yahveh wanted it to work, it would.

CHAPTER TWENTY-SIX

Four days later Jack, Laura, Mark, Sarah, David, Alexis, Charlie and Linda Wu, and Megan Cole walked out of the Crossfire Team side of the Sea Base and into the Advanced Research and Development Annex. They were dressed in full combat gear including Force Generators.

Laura stared at the futuristic aircraft that had the place of honor inside the huge hanger. It resembled the "Ghost" Autonomous aircraft but was smaller and sleeker.

The access door was open and the stairs were extended. Jack led the group up to the opening and waved each of the others on board. Then he climbed in and hit the button next to the door. The stairs collapsed into themselves and slid into a slot in the bottom of the door frame. The door came down and sealed against the hull.

Jack used four screws to attach a Force Generator to the bulkhead next to the door but didn't activate it.

There were sixteen comfortable looking seats in two groups of four on each side of a small aisle. The ten people stowed their gear and found a place to sit. Jack noticed he had to stoop over a bit as he stowed his gear then he took a seat in the front row next to Laura, Mark, and Sarah. There wasn't even a pretense of a cockpit on this aircraft. The large display screen attached to the front bulkhead was less than four feet from the outer nose of the airframe.

The screen lit up with a view of the hanger door in front of the aircraft and the dozen smaller screens below that which provided a large amount of visual and data in a myriad of colors. Two, three-foot high screens ran down each side of the interior of the hull from the front bulkhead to the last row of seats. These screens acted as windows in the sides of the aircraft.

The forward screen changed to show a trim man in his early thirties looking at them. "Hello Crossfire Team. I am Captain William C. Maxwell welcoming you back to the world of advanced aircraft.

The "Myth" is a generation beyond the "Ghost" in all aspects. This is the first cooperative effort between the

Israeli IDF Air Force and the Crossfire Team Air Force. The result surprised both of our organizations. It is very obvious to everyone on both teams that Yahveh God is leading the effort and it is beyond fantastic."

Captain Maxwell looked a bit bemused but carried on.

"The Myth is so sneaky it cannot be detected by any radar or sensor look up/down that is known today. It can fly farther, faster, and with an almost non-existent audible signature and visual footprint smaller than anything else flying today. There are two miniaturized CRAY computers on-board and the computer power and sensor arrays are more effective than all those on a new Arleigh Burke or Zumwalt class destroyer. If needed, the Myth can carry almost half of the firepower of one of those destroyers. I understand your mission and want to assure you that the Myth will not be taken captive or destroyed in this mission. As I have told you before with the Ghost and Ghost II, wring it out and bring it back in one piece. Good hunting."

The screen went back to the overview and data explosion on all events, vehicles, crews, etc.

The Team watched the screen as the hanger doors opened and the Myth taxied out onto the runway and immediately rolled forward and lifted into the air. It easily transited the flight corridor and exited the tunnel under the small island. Charlie pushed a switch on his tablet and the Force Generator connected to the plane activated in the "Special" mode. Besides its inherent stealth capabilities, the Myth disappeared from sight and became impervious to damage as it rapidly accelerated and flew up to a level three miles higher than the normal military aircraft corridor over the Med."

Mark was busy finishing his composition on their "conference" with the sitting U.S. President and his cabinet. He looked up at Jack and Laura. "Okay, if there are no major changes on their end, we should be able to walk into the underground Presidential Bunker. He will be there along with all his aides, the entire cabinet, and a sprinkling of Secret Service personnel. Our entire message will be delivered in less than ten minutes and then we depart."

Jack shook his head. "I still can't believe that we are going to casually break into the most secure room in the most secure building in the whole world to have a chat with the President and then exit without a battle."

Mark shrugged, "Well, he won't come to us, so..." Laura was praying as normal. Charlie had a portable version of the COMM/SEC department on his tablet. He looked up and made a thumbs up signal. "We are now insinuated into the Bunker security electronics and communications. I am going to have four different cameras on me to record all this."

Laura asked Jack, "Have you gone over your brief with the Lord as to what you'll say to the President?"

Jack smiled, "Yes, I have and we have His Heavenly permission to do all of this. This is very important to the Father's will for mankind. He loves all their soldiers too."

Charlie inserted a cable into a socket on his seat and took over the display on the front monitor. "Here is the secret access to the main tunnel leading to the back of the Bunker. He pointed up to a building near the intersection of Pennsylvania Avenue NW and 18th St NW. This is the building that we will disembark from the Myth under cover of darkness and a major, and shall we say, unexpected fireworks show over the Tidal Basin. We will be able to descend through the building and its secret second level basement without tripping any alarms. At that point we are in the tunnel system. I have rigged the alarm systems and the gates in the tunnels to let us pass while ignoring any vibrations or other sensor-exciting air movements, etc. As we reach the area of the Bunker there will be eight Secret Service Agents defending the outer door of the Bunker."

Mark took over the description of the operation. "Then, after the agents have been rendered unconscious for a sufficient amount of time we will gather at the front of the Bunker and Charlie will say "Open Sesame" and we will walk into the Bunker, closing the door behind us. If we've missed some new thing or anything at all, we will breach the Bunker as gently as possible and then render the internal Secret Service Agents unconscious. At that point we will appear and settle the occupants down. Jack will then give them their options. After that we will retrace our steps and leave the area. Please remember that every Agent, Police Officer, military personnel, and basically everyone else will sacrifice their lives to prevent our having our chat. Try not to injure or kill any of these people because that's not what we do and not what I think God wants us to do. Are we all clear on this?"

Charlie surrendered control of the video monitor and it resumed showing flight information. It was amazing the number of ocean-going ships below them that never knew they were flying over them. That applied equally to all of the countries naval forces sailing below them.

The Myth was so fast it had already reached the U.S. seaboard. At ground level the sun was setting in the west as the invisible plane headed for the U.S. Capital.

CHAPTER TWENTY-SEVEN

The Myth hovered invisibly over the roof of the building. After it used a knock-out gas that had no odor to render the three police officers and two tenant's unconscious it settled slowly down to the roof of the designated building. Charlie was armed with only a computer tablet. The rest of the Team carried only side arms.

Jack had everyone switch their Force Generators to the "Special" mode. Jack watched them all disappear. He activated the special field detector and eight faint shapes appeared on his combat field glasses. That was a necessary gift from Dr. Clashire so that they could detect each other as they moved invisibly.

The Myth was a larger faint shape as it rose almost silently against the bright sky fireworks over the Tidal Basin and disappeared from sight. The Team entered the roof-top stairwell. They went down the four stories to the ground floor and then they descended the first flight to the basement. Charlie checked his tablet and led them to the hidden entrance to stairs that led them to the secret second basement. Charlie entered several sequences on his tablet. The vault-like door opened on pneumatic hinges. From there, Charlie led them into and through eight long corridors, eight barricade gates and through dozens of defenses and alarms.

In the last corridor they saw the eight Secret Service Agents guarding the sealed blast door to the Bunker. An aerosol knock-out drug rendered all eight men unconscious. The Team gathered in front of the Bunker blast doors. Charlie typed in a command and the blast doors opened and the Team entered the anteroom to the Bunker conference room. Charlie closed the blast doors and sealed the Bunker again. Several of the Secret Service Agents approached the doors to see why they had cycled open and closed again. Not seeing anyone there they advanced to check the doors. All four of these men were treated to the knock-out drug and fell to the floor.

At that point the dozens of people in the conference room became concerned and some rose to their feet to see the fallen agents better. Jack switched his Force Generator to the "normal" position and suddenly appeared across the table from the President. Needless to say this created a lot of confused reaction and noise from the assembled crowd.

Jack smiled at the President. "Mr. President, my name is Jack Malone and I am the leader of the Crossfire Team. I, and my Core Team..." The other eight members appeared spaced carefully around the room. "...have come to discuss your concerted effort to destroy the Crossfire Team."

The President didn't even attempt to hide his anger or hatred of Jack. "You have made the stupidest move of your life busting in here. You will not leave here alive!"

Jack smiled at the man. "You know; it is funny that you would say that in that exact way. I had a demon from hell use the same words about me not too long ago before I killed it."

"First, Mr. President, we will not be killed by you or the forces you command. We are servants of the Creator of the Universe, Yahveh God, and He is not happy with your misguided efforts to turn the United States into a totalitarian fiefdom for your own uses under Marco Marino. Remember, his fate is the lake of fire. I also doubt that the American public or your international partners would appreciate your blind ambition and cruel violations of international and U.S. laws."

The President turned bright red in the face as his anger mounted. "I will not discuss anything with you...you terrorists! But, I will tell you that the human cattle that make up this country and those International Partners who are dumber than sticks mean nothing to me. I will ascend to being Marco Marino's number two man and I will rule over this country as I should, as a King or actually as a god!"

Jack looked at the powerful man with sadness. "Since you are not interested in compromise, here is a fact you need to remember. If you send the good, heroic, and honorable men and women of the armed forces against the Crossfire Team, they will not succeed. They don't deserve such callous treatment by you. We have not been, nor intend to be, enemies of America or the loyal, true

Americans that make up this once-great country. But, understand this. This is your one and only warning. You are fighting against God Himself by allying yourself with those demons that will destroy you and take your soul as soon as you are no longer needed."

Jack could sense of the mood of the people in the bunker. They felt like they were in the right and the Crossfire Team was in the wrong. Jack looked around at the hate and anger in the faces of the administration flunkies and said. "You people want to know who you are following and what the President's control looks like?"

Jack prayed that the Father would let the people in the room have a realistic vision of the demonic world and some of its inhabitants.

Everyone in the room except for the Team suddenly screamed, moaned, or passed out. Those that retained their consciousness fell to their knees or to the floor and pleaded for rescue. Even the look on the President's face showed the fear and dread that facing a real demon causes.

The whole vision lasted no more than two minutes but when it lifted the atmosphere in the room changed drastically.

Jack then said loudly. "That, ladies and gentlemen, is a very tiny view of hell and demons. That is the domain of Satan and he controls Marco Marino and through him, your President.

The President was still trying to catch his breath. He looked at Jack with a ray of hope. "Please, please, I didn't know. Help me escape this nightmare."

Jack nodded his head. We battle against the Lord of Hell and his demons constantly. Call off the battle against the only people here that are trying to help you.

"If you pursue this course then God will judge you and..." Jack looked around at the other people in the room. "...and those who serve you in this demonic effort to control this country. You are all at risk of the Holy anger of God and Hellfire."

"Remember your glimpse of hell. This is your only warning. Good day Mr. President."

The entire Team disappeared from sight and the Bunker blast doors opened again as the Team left. As they walked into the first hall, the blast doors closed and a massive hail of gunfire came from two directions and raked the walls, floor, and the ceiling.

Jack walked along with the other Team members and ignored the massive gunfire and the U.S. Army Delta Force soldiers who were attempting to kill them. Mark watched the attack and veered away from the other Team members. He passed invisibly by the riflemen and walked up to the Commander of the Delta Force, a Colonel named Frank Owens. Mark shifted to "Normal" mode and suddenly appeared in front of Colonel Owens. Mark smiled at the man and said, "You know Frank, you're a good man. If you ever want to work for the Commander of the Universe, call me. I'll introduce you to Him."

The Colonel looked at Mark for a few seconds. "Mark, I'm personally sorry that we're on opposite sides and I actually admire you, but I have to serve the elected Commander of these United States." He pulled out his service automatic and fired four rounds point-blank at Mark. Mark didn't move. Suddenly the automatic was ripped out of the Colonel's hand and thrown across the corridor.

Sarah appeared and stared at the Colonel. "I suggest you don't do that again! You are being misled and used as cannon fodder by this President and his administration. If you are truly Mark's friend then I will advise you, personally, not to come against us again. If you do, I hope you, personally, know Jesus because you will meet him then because I will introduce you to Him."

Mark grinned, "See you later, Frank" as both he and Sarah vanished from sight.

The Colonel shook his head. He told the troops to stand down. "All we're doing is wasting ammunition."

CHAPTER TWENTY-EIGHT

After leaving the various Secret Service and military personnel looking in all the wrong directions, the Team made its way back to the building and climbed to the roof. Now there were eight policemen and two snipers on the roof.

Mark looked out and saw an empty parking lot a block away from the next intersection to the north. He contacted the flight manager and rearranged the landing site of the aircraft to the parking lot. The Team made their way down to the ground level and over to the parking lot.

Mark watched as the ghostly image of the Myth settled to concrete in the parking lot. He walked to the door and Charlie typed in a code. The door opened and the stairs descended. Mark counted the other nine people into the aircraft and then joined them. The steps retracted and the door sealed closed. The Myth was preparing to depart when Sarah yelled, "Look out, they've found the plane!"

Mark looked at the video screen in time to see an APC race into the parking lot and speed directly at the plane. The APC smashed into the Force Generator field and came to an almost instantaneous stop. Soldiers flew out of the body of the APC and slammed into the field around the plane.

Jack said, "Can we take off and get out of here before there is more damage to those troops?"

Mark spoke into the air, "Myth ascend!" The plane tried to lift but the APC was resting on its starboard wing.

Jack walked over to the door and opened it. He stepped out and the door closed again. Jack walked around the nose of the aircraft and checked on the men on the ground. None dead, yet. He deactivated the "Special" mode and walked over to the upside down APC.

One of the men in the back of the APC managed to open the side hatch and crawled out. Seeing Jack, he said, "Please, help me! There are two men in here and they are hurt bad."

Jack stepped over to the trooper and moved him away from the wreck and laid him on the ground. Going back to the APC he met Mark, Charlie, and Sarah. "Help me get those two troops out of the back. That man said that they were hurt badly."

Mark half crawled and half hauled himself into the body of the APC. He found the two unconscious men and carefully moved them to the side hatch of the APC where Sarah and Jack moved them over to the area the first troop was at.

Charlie said, "There are two men in the front but they didn't make it."

Mark asked, "Is the APC clear of live troops?"

Charlie said, "As far as I can tell. There may be some under the APC but I doubt that they would be alive. Three of the five that flew out of the APC are alive but injured."

Jack told Mark, "Let's get the two bodies out of the cab and then move the APC off of Myth's wing."

It only took two minutes to remove the dead troops.

Jack then stood to the side of the APC and willed his Force Generator to move away from the plane. The APC groaned and then slid away from the Myth. Laura's voice came over the comm gear. "There are multiple vehicles coming this way and several helicopters and fast movers above us."

Jack saw Mark tending to the wounds on the first soldier and yelled, "Come on Mark, we have to go now."

Mark got up and ran to the door of the aircraft and hustled inside. Charlie, Sarah, and Jack entered and sealed the door. Jack said, "Wait a minute. I'm going to talk to our pursuers. I'll join you in a few minutes." Laura jumped up and said, "You're not going without me! The two of them opened the door and stepped out of the plane. The door sealed and Mark spoke into the air again, "Myth ascend to two thousand feet and avoid aircraft and missiles!"

The Myth lifted off of the parking lot and quickly rose straight upward. The Team on board switched their Force Generators to "Normal" mode and belted into their seats. The Myth tipped over to the right and began to move slightly away from the area.

Jack and Laura went back to the wounded men in the parking lot. Laura switched her Force Generator to

"Normal" and checked the injuries of the eight soldiers. With Jack's help she splinted the first man's broken arm and put an inflated air cushion around his neck. Gratefully the emergency supplies were available in the APC.

About that time two more APCs roared into the lot and came to a halt with their heavy machine guns aimed at the two Crossfire Team Members.

Jack covered the last of the eight men with a blanket to keep their body heat from being lost. He then stood up and walked over to the Major who had jumped out of the closer APC and walked over to the wounded men. He was careful to not come between the machine guns and the Team members.

On the Myth Mark commented, "Two of the F-22s are making a firing run on us. I'd like to know how they are detecting us solidly enough to get a firing solution."

The Team watched as the as the four Hellfire missiles slammed into the Force Generator field around the Myth and exploded. The Myth's electronics noticed that the explosions did not affect it and therefore ignored the attack and moved quickly to another position above the parking lot with Jack and Laura in it.

As Jack had almost reached the Major there was a massive explosion several thousand feet above the parking lot as the four Hellfire missiles hit the Force Generator field around the Myth. Jack watched the Myth move several hundred feet away from the explosion and knew it hadn't been hurt.

The Major had ducked and moved closer to the APC behind him as the sound of the explosions reached the people on the ground. He stood up and walked closer to Jack as Laura joined him.

"I am Major Underwood of the Capital Defense Forces and I am placing both of you under arrest for terrorism. Please turn around and place your hands behind you. I won't ask you twice."

Jack computed angles and calmly replied. "Major Underwood. We are not going to allow you to arrest us for any charges. But, since you seem to disagree I would suggest that you move your troops behind you to a safer location before you fire your machine guns. They could be hurt otherwise."

Above them the Myth calculated the paths of a dozen more ground to air and air to air missiles and avoided them all. Most of the missiles lost lock on due to the Myth's stealth design. Those missiles flew on to their self-destruct distance and exploded. There were three air-to-air heat seekers that had locked onto the exhaust heat of the Myth but hit the Force Generator field and exploded ineffectually.

The Major frowned but looked behind him and motioned the Special Forces personnel to get behind the APC. He turned back to Jack and Laura. "At least Mr. Malone let your wife step away from you."

Jack smiled. "Thank you for that courtesy Major but she is fine where she is. We are servants of God and your weapons will not harm us. Why don't you let them try so that temptation won't bother you anymore?"

The Major stood up straighter and said, "For the last time, Mr. and Mrs. Malone please surrender or we will be forced to fire."

Laura smiled at the officer. "Major, please go ahead and fire, you won't hurt us, I assure you."

The Major turned to the Machine Gunner. "Fire at will."

The vehicle mounted M2 .50 caliber heavy machine gun roared and sprayed the two people with forty-two rounds and then fell silent. The Major stood there not believing what he was seeing. Neither the man nor the woman had been hit or hurt.

Jack looked at the Major. "Sir, if you don't mind sparing the neighborhood of more collateral damage I would like to make a statement to the collective Armed Forces of the United States."

While the Major considered what to do, Charlie's voice was sounding in both Jack and Laura's ear buds. "Go ahead Jack, I've got the video of you on every broadcast and cable news channel and especially on the Armed Forces Radio and Network."

Jack looked directly at the APC Machine Gunner as he stated. "Men and women of the United States Armed Forces. The Crossfire Team used to work out of Colorado to defend the military, the FBI, and citizens from the enemy of all mankind, who you probably know better as Satan or the Devil. Satan has begun to defy God Almighty in these end time days and is bringing his demons directly into the human dimension to bring terror and destruction. We are one of many teams that God has anointed to fight these evil beasts. We are not your enemy but the misguided government of this country, who do not care how many of you have to die to serve their goals, is planning to send wave after wave of heroic and patriotic soldiers against us because we defy the commands of Marco Marino and his One-World-Government. We are servants of God and He protects us. The machine gun here is an example. Another example is the fact that two of us stood ten feet away from a two-megaton nuclear explosion without harm. But know this. God loves all of mankind including each and every one of you. Yet, if the government sends you against us as the President says he will, then you will not return home alive. This is not a threat, but it is a warning. God will protect us; will he protect you?" Thank you for listening. My name is Jack Malone and one of the Crossfire Team you might recognize is Mark Connelly, formerly a U.S. Navy Seal. He also asks that you understand our situation. We are no threat to the U.S. or its citizens or its soldiers. But we will defend ourselves. May we not meet in battle for your sakes."

Jack and Laura switched the Force Generators to "Special" and disappeared. They then looked upwards and "willed" themselves upward and away from the parking lot.

As they rose Jack saw the Myth close in on them. The plane matched their slow flight and the side door opened up. Standing on thin air at two thousand feet Jack had to smile as the stairs appeared. Jack willed his Force Generator to move to the door and he grabbed the hand rails inside the door and pulled himself into the body of the plane. He was followed almost immediately by Laura. The door closed and the Myth moved away quickly and turned straight up. It rose on twin pillars of blue fire and quickly broke the sound barrier. Four heat-seeking missiles locked onto the exhaust heat source but couldn't keep up with the rapidly climbing aircraft.

At eighty thousand feet the heat seekers had fallen so far behind that their explosions didn't even register as a problem at their altitude. The plane tipped over to the right and the speed indicator moved smoothly to the 9,000 MPH marking.

As the ride smoothed out Laura asked, "Do you think our warning will change the government's mind about sending the American military after us?"

Mark shook his head, "Nope, the delusional President is too far gone in his desire to rule the world as a king. In other words, he has completely accepted Marco Marino's demonic rule and his part in it. But, we can hope that the American people might change his mind to save their loved ones in the service."

Sarah shook her head. "I doubt that will happen. The President will deny that we were there, that he is a bad guy, etc. He will use our talk to make us out as the ultimate terrorists. By the time we can get our version of things to the public he will have flooded the airwaves so much the people won't know what to believe."

Charlie and Linda both laughed a little. Mark smiled, "Well, he is going to have an uphill battle to sell that to the people since we were able to broadcast the whole talk live while we were there."

Linda locked into one of the main cable channels and fed it to the main screen in front of them. A full color version of the President's rant was being rerun. Sarah smiled as she watched the President say, *"I will ascend to being Marco Marino's number two man and I will rule over this country as I should, as a King or actually as a god!"*

Linda switched to an international broadcast from Israel and Sarah heard the same information being broadcast with a Hebrew translation running across the bottom of the screen.

She looked at Jack and smiled. "Maybe he will have a hard time denying his real intentions."

CHAPTER TWENTY-NINE

David, Alexis, and Megan had been quietly discussing between themselves and David raised an interesting point to the leaders of the Team. "We were wondering how any of these arguments will affect Satan in the least. His whole thing is to do evil and destroy as many people as he can that love God. He hides in the dark and obscurity is his means of denying his part in things."

Jack was nodding his head. "That is true but, what we need to do is to threaten that obscurity in a big way to give us an acceptable edge to our argument that will persuade him to stop the government of the U.S. from using its military might in attacks against the Team."

Megan asked, "And how do we accomplish that? Satan has spent thousands of years convincing the population of the world that he isn't real and that he doesn't exist so that he can do his evil against mankind without being seen as the villain."

Jack looked at the three of them and asked, "Alexis, this is right up your alley with your psycho-war background. What would you do to achieve our goal to make the devil and his evil ways a household word?"

Alexis thought about that challenge for a bit. Then she brightened up and smiled. "We need to create a really effective advertising campaign that will sell the world on Satan's real goals, methods, and how he affects everybody. It would have to be classy, glossy, and full of undeniable examples. It would be great to have some interviews with real demons and illustrated with real cases of the evil Satan commits on everyday people, especially popular people that the world can identify with in their own lives. It would need to be distributed worldwide so that all people see it, understand it, and can relate to it. It needs to have a universally known and popular sponsor. This has to be someone that all people trust to tell them the truth. This campaign would have to be backed and distributed by every medium such as TV, Internet, radio, and movies. That is what I'd do to threaten the devil's obscurity."

Charlie asked, "So we need to find a high-class advertising group that doesn't worry about taking on Satan, has a lock on world-wide distribution, can provide a popular, and trustworthy, spokesman or woman, and can do all this in a short time. Is that about right?"

Alexis nodded, "That is what I think would make Satan listen to us and convince the Anti-Christ to not use good people to come against us."

Laura asked, "Why do you think the devil will worry about such a campaign when he can probably cripple or destroy it? Many marketing people and the "popular" entertainment people are not believers in God and are probably mostly in Satan's camp in the first place since one of their prime goals is making money for selfish reasons rather than moral goals. They would most likely listen to Satan's arguments rather than ours."

Jack thought about the discussion and spoke up. "Why don't we ask Yahveh about this and the way He would want us to do it?"

They all agreed and Sarah led them into praise and worship by singing hymns to the one true God in Heaven. Their worship deepened and Jack felt the heaviness that he knew meant God's Holy Spirit was with them. As Jack fell into heartfelt communion with a Father that loved him he sensed a presence of power. Opening his eyes, he saw Raquel sitting on nothing in front of the front screen, facing the Team.

Jack spoke first. "Hello Raquel, are you bringing us God's answer to our prayers?"

Raquel was in his Archangel persona and somewhat fearsome in appearance. When he smiled it modified his looks into a fearsome strength rather than a worrisome strength. "Hello Jack and everyone else. Yes, I was honored to bring you the Most High's answer to your prayers concerning how to influence Satan to help prevent Marco Marino's using the armies of the world to destroy your team. Now hear the word of God!

"My Children, Satan is not a human that can be swayed by influence or opinion. He is a purely evil spirit that only responds to a direct threat to his evil kingdom. He sees your team as my agents that stand against him and all that he wants to accomplish in your dimension. Even if

you could force him to make concessions he will disregard them as soon as he could nullify your force. He is going to do what evil he wants to do until I limit him or finally destroy him.

It is ambitious that you want to limit his use of people against you but it is also folly because he will not be persuaded. Your idea to expose him to the people of the Earth is based in your love for me and all my children. But, at this time in the last days before my Son returns it would only serve Satan to frighten the people of the world and elevate him more than he is already feared. I will place respect for your group in the hearts of the believers at all levels of the military and governmental officials throughout the world. Return to your base. I have work for you to defeat a terrible evil that is rushing upon the world as we speak. Stand in your faith in me and do not fear for I am with you forever."

Raquel nodded to Jack and vanished from sight.

Mark sighed. "Well, I guess that settles that. I also get the feeling that the Force Generators are going back into storage at this time." He looked at Sarah and grinned. "Back to the basics my dear."

Since they were over Israeli soil, Jack got up and turned off the aircraft's Force Generator.

CHAPTER THIRTY

As the Myth flew down the access airway toward the Sea Base Jack looked at Laura and asked, "What do you make of this last trip? We didn't really accomplish much except to convince one man that they were wasting ammo trying to kill us. We didn't change the President's mind about us and we exposed the Force Generators to a lot of people. Did we sin because we were essentially bullet-proof and could get away with it?"

Laura had been thinking about the same things for a while. She sighed, "I think we accomplished a great deal of good because we showed the world that we aren't the bad guys. We didn't expose the Force Generators because we told the world we were God's servants and that he would protect us, which he did. They don't know if there were angels protecting us or some other form of God's protection. We did set a precedent for any use of force against us that will have changed the way the U.S. military decides to treat or attack us. I don't think we sinned at all. God told us to resolve the problem of our having to war against good people. We definitely made that clear in your speech to the President that has been seen world-wide. I like the protection of the Force Generators, but, they are only to give us an equal chance against the enemy. Apparently the Father felt that we needed an equalizer in this case. Remember that God is all about love and we acted out of our love for our fellow soldiers to prevent our having to destroy them."

The squeal of the tires as the Myth touched down on the runway at the Sea Base signaled time to move out. Jack waited until the other people got their gear and exited the aircraft before doing the same. He unscrewed the Force Generator from the wall next to the door and put it into his backpack.

After he left, Charlie came back on and filled the four small holes in the panel left by the screws with a fast-drying putty that closely matched the color of the panel.

That afternoon, Jack got a call from Captain Maxwell of the Research and Development Group. "Hello Captain Maxwell, I want to thank you again for letting us use the Myth. It more than achieved our goals and we appreciate that. How can I help you?"

"You can tell me how in the world the Myth survived having an APC crash into it, flip over and land on its wing without leaving a scratch. Also, even more unbelievable, is that not one, but four Hellfire missiles hit the plane and detonated, again, without a scratch. We had to erase that data from the cybernetic brain of the aircraft so that it will not treat missiles as irrelevant the next time it is fired on."

Jack sighed, "If you have a little time I would like you to come over to our part of the base so I can tell you why those things happened. Meet me on the third level at the firing range, okay?"

An hour later the Captain was enlightened, discouraged and sworn to secrecy concerning the Force Generators. He bemoaned the fact that he couldn't use them in his next design. Jack prayed with him so that they could ask God about his desire. The Captain left without a Force Generator but much more committed to God and to his work. As he shook Jack's hand he smiled. "Well, you brought her back but I'm not sure we can integrate that particular performance with the other data due to the advantage of the Force Generator. The Lord definitely told me that Advanced Labs will see you again, soon. I am looking forward to your next "mission". Let me know if there are any particular upgrades or improvements you believe that the Ghost or the Myth could use."

CHAPTER THIRTY-ONE

Jack set a recall for the Core Team for six p.m. Tel Aviv time and sat at his desk in the War Room refining his notes concerning the coming meeting. There was a gentle knock at the War Room door and Jack turned to see Su Li standing there waiting for permission to enter.

Jack waved the diminutive Asian woman into the room and stared at her as she went to the seat next to him. He thought, "This isn't the same Su Li I knew before. She would have just walked in and sat down and dared me to speak about it."

Jack smiled at her and asked what he could do for her.

Su Li looked into his eyes and asked. "Okay, what did you do to me?"

Jack realized she was talking about her *"it didn't happen"* trip to Heaven. "I prayed for you but other than that I didn't do anything to you. What's the concern?"

She lowered her eyes and then looked back at him. "I don't know. I do know I am not myself anymore. I have a hole in my memory and since then I think I've lost my edge, my drive, or something. What can you tell me about this?"

Jack prayed for direction and definitely heard Rose say; "Tell her about her death and rebirth. It was for the better for her. The Most High took what was meant for bad by the enemy and made it good. She is now in synchronization with her spiritual self and can now grow in the Lord."

Jack sat back and stared at Su Li for a minute. "Do you remember when Captain Eckhart from the SOG was killed along with several other SOG personnel travelling with Captain Eckhart to his father's funeral because the demons made the plane crash?"

Su Li nodded.

"Do you also remember that God restored him and everyone concerned, including the pilot and the aircraft because they weren't supposed to die?"

She nodded again.

113

Jack smiled, "That "hole" in your memory is when your Tilt Rotor was destroyed on the ground during the recent battle over the Mossad Headquarters. That blast caused you to die later that day. But, you were killed by a dead man which Satan reanimated just long enough to kill you. Because of that illegal operation, God has restored you and everything that was destroyed. You were taken to Heaven and by that night you were restored to us without any memory of your trip to Heaven that you were not supposed to take."

Su Li digested that information and nodded. "Then why am I not as driven as I was before to accomplish everything I do?"

Jack reached over and took her smaller hands in his. "Because during your time-out God refined you and removed the fear and anxieties you were still harboring. He did that in compensation for your having to go through a death sequence that was not yours to travel."

Jack listened to the word of God that dropped into his spirit and nodded his head. "You still had uncertainty about your ability to fill your role with us or even just in life that you were unaware of. These fears and anxieties from the demonic realm drove you to maximize everything you did to convince yourself as well as the rest of us that you were worthy of everything you have achieved. Abba says that you are worthy and removed the doubt and uncertainty. Now, you can grow in your faith knowing that the Creator of the Universe knows that you are worthy of all of it. Now, you don't have to prove it to yourself or anyone else. Accept it as the Lord's peace and rest assured you can now excel in everything you do and even reach greater achievements."

Su Li sampled her peace and realized that her present concern was the enemy trying to unsettle her again. She prayed silently that Yahshua would use the power of the Holy Spirit to burn up all of the efforts of the enemy to put the chains of fear and uncertainty back on her. She confessed the sins and that door was closed forever by the Father. The concerns faded into nothingness. She looked up at Jack and smiled a confident smile. "I thank you, Jack, I doubt if you know that as the Priest of this outfit you are wonderful. You have made me realize that I am whole and God loves me."Su Li smiled and stood up.

Jack stood up as she did and he hugged her. "Welcome home, Su Li."

Su Li danced out of the War Room almost knocking Laura over as they met in the doorway. Su Li fiercely hugged her spiritual mentor and kissed her on the cheek. Smiling she said, "God is Great!" and took off at a run.

Laura was grinning as she walked up to Jack. "I saw her before and suggested she talk to you. That must have been one great pep-talk you gave her."

Jack pointed upward and shrugged his shoulders. "Not me, my love, not me. I was just the messenger."

CHAPTER THIRTY-TWO

Iris Jakobson listened to the report of the three officers of the IDF for the second time. She shut off the recorder and looked at her new Senior Assistant Director with a worried look. "Well, Ehud, what do you think about that summation?"

Ehud Torvil frowned, "I think we may have a major problem on our hands and no way to get a handle on it."

Iris sighed, realizing that she had been the Director of the Mossad less than three weeks and the list of challenges kept growing. She was convinced that the job would wear her out if they didn't start having successes soon. She brightened up as she thought for a minute. "Don't be too sure about that Ehud. I believe I know someone might have that handle you believe is missing."

She put in a call to Jack Malone and requested his presence as soon as possible at her office.

Thirty minutes later Jack and David Zahavy were shown into her office. She smiled at the two men. "Please, sit down gentlemen. I knew we were going to have a working arrangement that would be very active. I have a new problem for you that as the Americans would say, should be right up your alley."

Jack smiled at the woman that ran one of the most effective spy groups in the world. "Why don't you tell us about the "problem".

Iris shook her head, "one of our nuclear weapons, which we don't admit we have, has turned up missing. The leaders of the IDF feel that the weapon was stolen by three of their own technicians who have now dropped off the face of the world. I believe that this theft is somehow related to the attack on this headquarters two weeks ago."

David asked, "Why do you believe that Director?"

I believe that because all three of those technicians were here at the time of the attack. They reported that they were able to disengage from the attack and return to their base. But, they were seen in the vicinity of this office during the battle. You two were here and know what was happening at that time. I don't know how they could have gotten away from the battle and left without encountering any of the enemy agents or the demons that were outside this building."

Jack had his suspicions but wanted to confirm them. "Director, I think we need to some higher power help to determine what happened to those men and what has happened to the weapon. Shall we pray?"

Iris nodded her head. "I have this room locked down so that we won't be disturbed."

Jack looked at David, "then let us lock down the spiritual approaches."

Jack prayed for divine covering by the Lord Yahshua so that the enemy couldn't intervene in their prayer time and eavesdrop on their meeting in any manner. He then began to praise the Father and declare the promise that God had given man in James 1:5-8."[5] *If any of you lacks wisdom, you should ask God, who gives generously to all without finding fault, and it will be given to you.* [6] *But when you ask, you must believe and not doubt, because the one who doubts is like a wave of the sea, blown and tossed by the wind.* [7] *That person should not expect to receive anything from the Lord.* [8] *Such a person is double-minded and unstable in all they do."*

The three people fell silent and waited on the Lord.

Iris had never before felt the power in a prayer that accompanied this prayer. She rested in great hope that the Creator of the Universe would respond to their request.

A voice of great power spoke and the three people opened their eyes and beheld the angel Caleb in his warrior persona. His white robes were bright as sunlight and his eyes burned with fire. "You do well to seek wisdom Jack Malone; this is a very dangerous situation. The Most High commends all three of you on your faith. Now hear the word of Yahveh. *"Once again the enemy of all mankind is crossing boundaries I have not given him permission to cross in his desire to destroy man's faith in Me. Satan has obtained this weapon of destruction to profane the name of My people and throw the world into a global war. The Mossad and the Crossfire Team alone must stop this evil. My messengers want to fight alongside your people. But this cannot be at this time. Preventing this evil will be the sternest test of your faith and capabilities. Pray for strength as you seek to uncover this plan. You must face both demons and humans on your own. This time even I cannot reveal the purposes or plans of the enemy. I cannot allow you to use the Force Generators that you have this time. I call upon each person in the Mossad and the Crossfire Team to protect My people and the city I love."*

Caleb finished delivering the word of the Most High but did not leave like normal. His eyes locked on that of Iris Jakobson as he said, "Satan seeks to change the prophetic future and blame the destruction of much of the Holy City on Israel and their allies. There is little time left before he strikes. As the Most High said, I cannot intervene this time." Then he disappeared and the room was darker with his going.

Iris Jakobson sat there in a state of shock as Jack ended their prayer with thanks to the Father in the name of Yahshua. The world was spinning around and she was feeling very lost and confused. Then Jack placed his hands over hers on the desk and her mind cleared up from the anointing Jack carried. He prayed for the peace of God to fill her and remove any confusion. The power that flowed through Iris washed away any doubt or concern. Her thinking returned to normal and she relaxed. Looking up at Jack she said, "That was the most profound and awesome thing that has ever happened to me. Everything else pales into unimportance and I am left full of joy and contentment."

Jack grinned at her. "We've all had that reaction before. After a lifetime of seeing things one way and suddenly realizing the truth isn't quite what one thought it was, prayer is necessary. We had to ask the Father to realign your thinking and move you into your new reality."

David nodded, "Director, I think I have an idea of what has transpired and where this action is headed."

Iris stepped into her new reality with her faith firm in understanding who was in charge of her destiny and that of the Israeli people. "Please, David, explain your understanding."

David looked for agreement from Jack. Jack nodded. David took a deep breath. This batting words around between two top leaders who were just anointed by Yahveh was heady stuff. "I believe that the entire attack on the Mossad Headquarters was to allow Satan's demons to acquire the identities of those three IDF technicians. The three men were replaced by three demons acting as them. They probably studied all three men for months if not years just to be able to imitate them properly. I would hazard a guess that the three original technicians are dead. The demons assumed their likenesses and then arranged for the theft of the nuclear device. Other demons shielded the device so that real technicians that were on duty did not detect the theft. Am I right in thinking that the three men cannot be found now?"

After the Director nodded, David took a breath and focused on the next part of his theory. "I believe that after the demons removed the device from the base they took it directly to the target while it was still covered. I think their target is the Temple Mount. I also believe that they want to detonate the weapon on the Temple Mount for three purposes. First, they can influence the world against the Israelis because the bomb will give off the identifiable signature that it was an Israeli weapon. Second, using this wanton destruction they can inflame the millions of Muslims worldwide by the destruction of their most sacred place as an ultimate insult and act against their religion. Third and lastly, they hope to destroy the ability of God to build the third temple on the Temple Mount, thus denying the prophesy of Daniel 11:31 to be fulfilled." David quoted from the book of Daniel, Chapter 11, and verse 31:

³¹*"His armed forces will rise up to desecrate the temple fortress and will abolish the daily sacrifice. Then they will set up the abomination that causes desolation.*

"This passage refers to the act of the Anti-Christ seating himself in the temple and declaring himself God on Earth."

Jack shook his head, "If that is what they are planning then we have a real problem. It won't be easy trying to find, deactivate, or remove the bomb there. The Muslims won't let anyone other than other Muslims on the Temple Mount. They especially won't let Jews or Christians up there. Even if we are trying to save their mosque."

Iris frowned, "YHVH will make a way."

Jack smiled faintly. "While that is true, I find that when He tells us to do something we have to do our best to accomplish what He has instructed us to do. Also, the angel Caleb delivered YHVH's message which said that it was up to us this time."

Iris sighed, "Okay, what we have here is a plausible theory that we need to verify before we try to convince other people. How do we verify it?"

David thought about that. "I suggest we "invite" some of Marco Marino's people who would be in the know and inquire about these things."

Iris chuckled, "Time hasn't changed you David. I agree, and I think I know just the people we need to "invite". Since the problem of demons acting as Mossad personnel indicated that my group could have some leaks right now, let's use Crossfire Team members to provide the "invitees" and an unknown location, so that we have a chance to talk to them without distractions."

"Who do you have in mind?" Jack asked.

The Mossad Director took out a sealed package from one of the drawers of her desk. She slid out the contents and spread them out in front of Jack and David.

Iris Jakobson pointed to three pictures. She pointed to the first picture. "This Amasa Meshek, a one-year appointee to the Kinnesit. He promotes himself as a conservative of the Lukid party. In reality, he is a solid backer of Marco Marino and a devotee of the One-World-Government."

"The man in the middle picture is Yoni Greenberg, Amasa's financial backer and companion. He is sort of a middle man between the OWG and the Kinnesit and works through Amasa. Yoni arranges things so that they go the way Amasa wants them to go, you know, a political fixer."

"The last picture is that of Muna Meshek. She is Amasa's sister and we believe she is also his assassin. We also think that she was trained as an assassin in Russia. She handles the wet work and is very proficient at it. She is also very clever. We know of several people that she has killed but we have no solid evidence to arrest her on. She leaves no witnesses, no forensic evidence, and has been able to avoid our surveillance, elint, and even public cameras when she is dealing death."

CHAPTER THIRTY-THREE

Jack looked at the photo of the attractive black-haired woman. She reminded him a great deal of Raisia Ivanova, the Russian trained assassin who worked for the Omicron Cartel. Change Muna's hair color to red and she would have been a close match for Raisia. Jack showed the photo to David. "I think we've fought this war before."

Jack considered the idea of the Team kidnapping these people for a one-way consultation. "We don't have any proof that these people are doing anything wrong. Or, that they have any involvement in the theft of the nuclear weapon. How can we justify our action if they aren't guilty?"

Iris smiled at Jack, "Ooops?"

David laughed, "We are usually not wrong about their guilt; it is the political outrage and public denunciation that concerns us. I have done this many times before and only twice did I have to make apologies and make things right because the people were actually innocent of wrong doing." David recalled one of those embarrassing times.

-----------------------******-----------------------

The night was unusually dark as David waited with a large select team of IDF and Mossad troops inside the trailer of an eighteen-wheeler being used as a pre-raid-base. The information on this operation came from three different terrorists and matched so closely there could not have been a mistake.

As the team leader, David was listening to three different communications networks and watching a half-dozen video input feeds surrounding the small building that was the center of their attention.

According to the Intel there were approximately thirty terrorists inside the building which was being used as a bomb making factory. The men running the place were some of the more vicious bombers the Mossad had been looking for around the world. This operation could be a major strike to the terrorist organization whose name, in English would be Night Hawks.

Everything would be recorded on video to prevent any legal loopholes that would allow the terrorists to avoid prosecution.

The four-hour surveillance preceding the raid had not identified any of the known terrorists in Israel. But there were watchers at windows and guards at the doors. Because they had no real positive Intel the Mossad was going in, starting with stun guns and Tazers rather than live ammunition.

David got the "GO" signal and sent the troops out of the truck with the admonition to try to catch them all alive rather than dead.

Flash Bang grenades and stun guns cleared the way into the building with little or no trouble. The forty troopers and ten Mossad agents surged through the three floors quickly and efficiently. The "All Secure" signal came after less than twenty minutes. The suspects were all rounded up in a large room on the ground floor. David was concerned because no bombs and no weapons were found so far.

David got a real shock when he walked into the room. All the suspects were handcuffed and on their knees with twenty-five IDF soldiers watching them. That wasn't the shocking thing. Twenty of the "suspects" were teen-agers.

There were seven adults and David had three of them taken to separate rooms for interrogation. He sat down at a table with one of the three guarded men seated across from him.

Looking at the man that was probably in charge, David asked him. "What is your name and are you in charge of this operation?"

The man looked sullenly at David and gave him his name. Then, frowning, the man asked what David was doing assaulting him and the others with heavily armed soldiers.

David asked him again. "What is going on here?"

The man stared at David for a minute and said sarcastically. "We are a diabolical supply team chartered to provide food for two thousand Holocaust survivors in Tel Aviv. If you don't believe me then you can ask the man who hired us to do this. That would be the Mayor of Tel Aviv who should be here any minute!"

A multitude of emotions washed across David as he realized the colossal blunder of which he was in charge. He asked the man why they were hidden here and had lookouts and door guards if everything was so legal.

The man suddenly realized how incriminating their operation must look to someone who wasn't in on the Mayor's little surprise party. "Well, I'm guess I can see how it would look, but why didn't you just have someone with a badge knock on the door and ask what was going on?"

David frowned, "That would be fatal for the asker if you had turned out to be a terrorist bomb factory as you were identified as by several completely individual terrorists."

The man fell quiet. David asked the other team leaders if this information was verified and the men all agreed. They had found the assembly and processing of food packets and most dangerous thing in the building was a rock-and-roll station on an IPad.

David had the suspects released and the troops dismissed. He had the other agents and IDF officers take the troops and disperse. As the processing got back to work David sat there and waited for the Mayor.

Since no one had gotten hurt other than several stunned students and some major headaches from the flash-bangs the Mayor was willing to overlook the mistakes and actually congratulated David for the efficiency of his troops and the fact that the suspects had been processed, and released, without any sign of brutality. He had been a police officer himself and could see why the raid had been called. David's superiors hadn't been as agreeable. David had to smile.

-----------------------*******-----------------------

Jack and David said goodbye to Iris and headed back to the Sea Base. David looked at Jack as they rode in the back of the Mossad SUV. "I am not sure I am correct in my determination of what is to transpire."

Jack sighed, "That concerns me too. I had a catch in my spirit when you laid that out. Something isn't right and

I want the Core Team to help us determine what that catch signifies."

After he walked into the War Room where the entire Core Team was waiting, Jack played back the recording of the discussion Iris Jakobson had with David and him. He read by his notes of Caleb's information including the word of God they had received. Lastly he replayed David's conclusions.

"This is what we are up against as a Team working in conjunction with the possibly compromised Mossad. I want each or you alone, or in sub-teams to come up with your idea of what is happening, what is expected, by when, and I need it in four hours. Be back here at five o'clock sharp."

CHAPTER THIRTY-FOUR

At precisely five p.m. Jack walked into the War Room. He looked at the assembled Core Team and noticed the focused attention each person was giving to the matter at hand

Besides himself and Laura there was Mark and Sarah Connelly, David and Alexis Zahavy, Charlie and Linda Wu, Mike White, Su Li, Megan Cole, Ethan Reaper, Carol Moffet, and Elon Lukin. The possible destruction of Jerusalem, let alone their team, was to be decided by these fourteen Judeo-Christians and Messianic Christians.

The Core Team's many comments and thoughts had been collected into one major view of the situation.

Alexis had been chosen as spokesperson. She threw the combined input from Jack up on the main screen. She looked at him for approval to start. He nodded.

She turned on her laser pointer and started at the top. "First, upon examination we have concerns about the input Director Jakobson gave you. Look at the statements she made." $$$$$

"One of our nuclear weapons has turned up missing."

"This is a declarative statement without facts. Which weapon was taken? When was it taken? How does the IDF think the weapon was stolen and taken away from the base?"

"The leaders of the IDF feel that the weapon was stolen by three of their own technicians who have now dropped off the face of the world."

"What investigation was done? What possible ways of stealing the weapon and dropping off the face of the world were considered?"

"I believe that this theft is somehow related to the attack on this headquarters two weeks ago."

"I am on the Director's side but don't know why she would connect the two incidents. What are her thought patterns that brought her to that conclusion?"

"I believe that because all three of those technicians were here at the time of the attack. They reported that they were able to disengage from the attack and return to their base. But, they were seen in the vicinity of this office during the battle. You two were here and know what was happening at that time. I don't know how they could have gotten away from the battle and left without encountering any of the enemy agents or the demons that were outside this building."

"Perhaps this was her reasoning. But, she herself was outside the building with Mark and or the General of the IDF. We can suppose that she had independent reports of their presence and then? She admitted that she didn't know how they could have gotten away. Are we sure that we have the real Iris Jakobson?"

"Now, we come to the Word of God delivered by Caleb. Everyone believes this is truly the Word of God but, what did God tell us in this Word?"

" ...the word of Yahveh. "Once again the enemy of all mankind is crossing boundaries I have not given him permission to cross in his desire to destroy man's faith in Me. Satan has obtained this weapon of destruction to profane the name of My people and throw the world into a global war. The Mossad and the Crossfire Team alone must stop this evil. My messengers want to fight alongside your people. But this cannot be at this time. Preventing this evil will be the sternest test of your faith and capabilities. Pray for strength as you seek to uncover this plan. You must face both demons and humans on your own. This time even I cannot reveal the purposes or plans of the enemy. I cannot allow you to use the Force Generators you have either. So, I call upon each person in the Mossad and on the Crossfire Team to protect My people and the city I love."

"The first statement is God's statement – Satan is cheating again to destroy man's faith in Yahveh. That is normal."

Alexis moved her pointer down on the screen. "It states that the Mossad and the Crossfire Team "alone" must stop this evil. What about the IDF? We cannot conclude anything about the use of the SOG. They are actually part of our team, so that is probably all right."

"The statement that His messengers (angels) want to fight alongside the Mossad and our team but they cannot do it "this time." This indicates that God's angels want to help us but are restricted "this time". "And God's statement that even He cannot reveal the purposes or plans of Satan. Obviously, there has been an agreement made between God and Satan that restricts God's action in the event "this time". "The Core Team agrees that it is probably a "Quid-pro-quo" or a "This for that" agreement. We feel that we, and especially Mark, have enraged Satan so much that he is willing to give up something important to God so that he has leverage. It might be a near-future attack or slaughter. In return, God has agreed to stay out of the action "this time" to allow Satan some advantage."

Alexis turned off the screen image. "After some brief discussion, we have concluded several things. First, this attack may be being used by Satan to set-up or destroy both our team and the new leadership of the Mossad. Yes, the nuclear signature would identify the weapon as Israeli, but, we think Satan wants to make the world believe that we, not the Israelis, used the weapon to destroy something Holy and probably in Jerusalem. To accomplish that Satan needs bodies, our bodies, alive or dead to prove that it was our team that did it."

"Second, we believe that this is being set up as a double-ended trap. We go where we think the weapon will be used and are captured and videoed for the Public Relations end of the case while the bomb destroys us and whatever the enemy wants to pin on us. It could just be a large population of innocent people. Or, we are lured to the wrong place and the bomb is used somewhere else and we are still set-up as the perpetrators, or so that we watch the explosion and there will be tape at eleven."

Alexis sat down and finished up with. "Whatever is going on here, we believe that we are the target and Satan has given up something important to keep God and the angels out of it to get the jump on us. I personally believe that Satan would give up half of his domain to get his claws on Mark. WOW, General! You can really irritate the demonic powers when you get the chance."

Mark nodded, "I think you're right about that. We need to find a way to sort out the reality of this thing and we have to do it very quickly. I am quite sure that Satan will try to trap us. But, if it doesn't work he will still blow up the bomb to point at Israel and kill all the people he can and still come at us again later. It is our mission to stop him in either case."

Jack held up his hand and silence fell. "We cannot pray this time and expect our usual assistance in the spiritual world. So, let's do it the old fashioned way, let's see if we can't find that bomb on our own."

Later that evening, Jack, Laura, Mark and Sarah were sitting hunched over a conference room table and tossing ideas around.

Mark threw his pen down on the pile of hen scratches on the numerous pieces of paper and pads. "Okay, I am just about convinced we will only find that bomb if I act as bait and see if we can't get old pointy-ears to act on it."

Sarah looked at her husband and wondered if he had actually lost it this time. "You are crazy! You know that Satan can't wait to get a shot at you when God can't interfere. So you want to go to his place and thumb your nose at him in hopes he'll give up the bomb to get you. OF COURSE he will! Then you'll be dead and he'll just go ahead and use the bomb, or he'll get another bomb. That is probably the stupidest thing you've ever come up with. Well, NO! I forbid it."

Mark looked at his wife like she must have just lost the little control thingy that kept her from losing her mental bearings. He said, "You think I'm going to let that old snake get me? You forgot about my secret weapon."

Her right eye-brow climbed to a new height on her forehead. "Exactly what secret weapon do you have?"

Mark smiled, "Why, you guys of course. Satan doesn't stand a chance. Who are you, and I, in Yahshua? We are Yahveh's kids! Satan is just God's whipping boy, have you forgotten that?" He shook his head and sat back in his chair and watched her.

Jack smiled, "You know of course, he's right. I don't believe that the Creator of the Universe would let Satan negotiate Him out of taking care of His kids."

Laura rolled her eyes. "You know that doesn't mean Mark or any of us will live through this. Okay Mark, how do you want to play this?"

Mark chuckled, "I think I need to call the old snake out in a showdown. My rules, not his. I'm betting myself and he has to bet the nuke. Winner takes all."

Sarah shook her head. "He won't obey the rules and he will definitely cheat. How are you going to beat him? At what are you going to challenge him to do?"

Mark stretched out his six foot-two-inch frame in a big yawn and put his hands behind his head. "I'm going to let it be known in the spiritual world that I'm challenging Satan to a sword fight and he'll have to respond or every little demon in his domain will know he's a coward if he doesn't come out to play. They all know he will cheat, but, we know he'll cheat, so we will be expecting that and planning for it."

CHAPTER THIRTY-FIVE

Mark went to the arboretum to map out his plans. He first prayed protection from any source or power that could spy on him or his plans. Then, he prayed for wisdom and favor in designing his showdown with the Prince of Evil. He made a short phone call and then two more calls. Binding up his sheets and notebooks he went to find Jack.

Finding Laura in the War Room he asked where Jack was. Laura explained that Jack was at the Mossad HQ building with the Director working on their mutual problem. Mark nodded, "Okay, if he looks for me tell him I am going to go get some equipment for my grand plan. I'm going to drop off the grid for most of this evening and tomorrow morning. I don't want our automated locator system or my phone's GPS giving away where I am going to be. I'll straighten this out with Sarah before I go."

Mark then found Sarah working on her swordsmanship in the large workout area of the gym. She looked really sharp and cute too. Mark interrupted her and told her the same thing and assured her that he would keep at least one Team member with or near him for protection. Having only one hand free she used it to hug him. She kissed him and told him to be safe. He handed her his medallion and his cell phone and left her to her practicing.

The next afternoon he returned and claimed his stuff and took Sarah, Jack, and Laura with him as he visited IDF General Haim Levy who was the Chief of the General Staff.

Mark shook hands with the IDF leader and sat down across the desk from the man. General Levy was a friend of the Crossfire Team and knew all of them well. He waved the others to seats. "Now, what can I do for the Crossfire Team?"

Mark smiled, "A small thing General. I'd like to borrow one of your non-existent one megaton nuclear warheads and a way to detonate it."

To say that the look on the General's face was surprised would have been an understatement. Shocked might have been closer. After blinking several times, the General grinned. "This is a joke, right?"

Mark shook his head, "No Sir, it is definitely not a joke. I need it to take it to hell and threaten Satan with it. If I don't use it, I'll bring it back in good shape. If I do use it, then the Team will replace the funds needed to get you a new one."

The General digested that for a few seconds and then, noting that the other three members also looked shocked, said, "So, you want to borrow a hypothetical one megaton nuclear warhead from me so you can take it to a realm off of the Earth and use it to "threaten" Satan with it? Have I got that right?"

Mark nodded his head, "Yes, Sir. That's the request."

The General thought for a few minutes and then asked Mark, "When do you have to have it?"

Mark shrugged, "Tomorrow morning would be good."

The General swung around in his chair and looked at Jack. "General Malone, do you believe that General Mark Connelly is in his right mind? And, if so, do you back him up as far as the replacement costs?"

Jack smiled, "Yes General Levy. I do trust Mark to do what he is saying and yes, I'll pick up the bill if he damages it."

The General stared at Jack. "You know we're talking about a half million U.S. dollars."

Jack shrugged his shoulders, "I can get you the cash or a cashier's check in two hours. You can hold it until we see if we need to buy it."

The General sat there looking at Mark for a minute. "Tell me why you need to do this thing."

Mark said, "This is the only way that we can prevent your missing nuclear weapon from being detonated in Jerusalem in the next few days."

Laura spoke up. "General, pardon me, but you can check with the Director of the Mossad as to this problem."

The General looked at the telephone on his desk. "Oy Vey! No, I must make this decision. But, I must have the Prime Minister's approval to use this hypothetical weapon."

The General called the PM. The PM called Jack. Jack set up a three-way conversation and explained the need to prevent Israel from being blamed for the destruction of the

Temple Mount. He also explained the precautions the Team was going to take to keep it out of the hands of terrorists or anyone else for that matter.

The PM agreed to the request, the General ordered a special delivery and then asked Mark. "How in G-d's name are you going to get this into the demonic dimension?"

Mark smiled, "I'm going to have Satan bring it in for me."

Jack shook his head, "But, how are you going to get it back out if you don't use it?"

Mark frowned, "Hopefully, the "one time" will be over and we can ask the Father to bring it back out. Failing that, then I'll detonate it so that it won't fall into the wrong hands."

Sarah shook her head, "And what about you, dear husband?"

Mark grinned, "Then I'll see you after I find a way home."

Jack grinned back. "That shouldn't be too hard. By then if Satan can't kill you he'll send you back just to get you out of his realm."

The General stared at the four of them. "You people do know this thing weighs over a half a ton. How you plan to move it, by backpack?"

Mark shook his head, "No. By a special six-wheel drive "Mule" that we happen to have on our base. We will also need a way to detonate it."

The General shook his head. "I told them to include the test panel. That will allow you to roast all the marshmallows you want to in a two cubic mile area."

After bidding the General farewell, the Team returned to their Sea Base and awaited the delivery of their own, personal nuclear weapon. Jack turned to Mark. "I just had the horrible thought that this is exactly what Satan wants us to do so that he can get this weapon and it'll be our fault."

Mark shook his head. "I've already thought of that."

CHAPTER THIRTY-SIX

The weapon was delivered by a special weapons team of IDF soldiers. Once it was signed for it became the Crossfire Team's problem.

Mark had it brought down to the Sea Base and secured in a very special vault with numerous video and live guards. The SOG was very attentive to the well-being of the nuclear weapon. Mark then got everybody fitted in their new combat armor. Jack asked, "What's this? I didn't know that we had new body armor."

Mark grinned, "This is a new arrangement I had created just for this trip. I guarantee you that you'll love it."

Sarah looked at Mark seriously. "Okay, Mr. Fixit, how do we get in touch with Old Nick and get him to get us and your little toy into his dimension?"

Mark looked at his wife. "Oy, married a couple of years and yet so feisty. Watch and learn O' young one.

For the next four hours Mark made preparations for a return trip to the demonic dimension. Everyone went to bed for the night. The next morning Mark had the nuke carefully packed into the chamber on the back of the six-wheel "Mule" and he held up three straws. "One of us has to stay here and man the fort. I've debated and thought this thing over and decided the only way to pick two of the three of you is by random straw draw. The short straw doesn't get to visit beautiful downtown hell."

Laura put her hand over Mark's bigger one. "Don't concern yourself Mark. I am going to stay here. You three make a better coordinated team and my major weapon is prayer which is not valid in this action. But, you had better bring my love back to me or even hell won't be big enough for you to hide in from me."

Mark smiled and pulled the center straw out and gave it to her. It was shorter than the other two. Jack, Mark, and Sarah suited up with their new body armor and M-8s with all the trimmings. They walked into the middle of the large area in the armory and the Mule dutifully followed them one step behind.

Mark made sure everything was ready and yelled into the air "ROSE!"

There was a sudden swirling of brilliant white and gold and the angel Rose appeared in front of Mark. "Yes, Mark, what do you require that doesn't go against what the Most High declared?" She didn't look really happy at the summons.

Mark smiled, "This is perfectly within the bounds of the agreement. Please use whatever communications you have to tell the Ogre in charge of the Demonic Realm that Mark Connelly, two acquaintances and their vehicle would like to be transported to the demonic dimension to have a shootout with Satan."

Rose looked at Mark pretty much the way IDF General Levy had looked at him the day before. She smiled, "I take it you are going to drive Satan totally crazy this time?"

Mark said, "Yeap, right off the chart. I Promise."

Rose checked with someone, possibly God Himself, and nodded her head. "It seems that Satan is agreeable, which is good because even the Most High can't be involved in moving you into the demonic dimension. I am intrigued in the mayhem you are about to cause. Anyway, my prayers will go with you." Raising her right hand, she said an unpronounceable word and the Sea Base disappeared to the three team members.

Rose looked at Laura standing there by herself. "I'm sorry Laura, the Most High said to let them go."

Laura laughed with the angel. "Be of good cheer Rose. All Hell is about to break loose in the demonic dimension."

CHAPTER THIRTY-SEVEN

The three Team members suddenly found themselves in the deep ominous twilight-like dimness of the demonic dimension. Mark reached over and used his thumb and forefinger to squeeze the collar of Jack's body armor just below his chin. He watched with satisfaction as a pin-head green LED lit up just below the switch. He then repeated the operation with Sarah's body armor. He looked at Jack and grinned as he winked. His green LED was already glowing.

There was a great deal of chattering, screaming, and yowling as hundreds of demons charged the three humans. Mark nodded his head and all three of the warriors began to pray and their golden and silver armor exploded into existence along with their shields and swords of the esteem of Yahveh.

This caused the demons to slide to a halt several yards away from the Crossfire Team members. Mark ignored the demons and went back to the Mule and checked two readouts. There were no problems and Mark smiled and walked to the front of their group. "Where is Satan?"

The floor and the walls shook and the lighting dimmed. In a burst of fire Satan appeared before Mark with three major sub demons.

Mark yawned like he was bored. Satan thundered "Now that you are here, Mark Connelly, let's get on with your little game so that I can end your existence once and for all!"

Mark looked at Satan and knew that the Father in Heaven had covered all three of them in heavenly protection that prevented the old snake from cursing them or putting assignments on them.

Mark looked at the ultimate evil in the earth and said, "We realize that this stealing of the Jewish nuclear weapon was simply another ploy of yours to get us involved. I thought that I would cut to the chase and have a personal showdown to save us time and effort. My challenge, my rules, is that all right with you?"

Satan laughed, "Perhaps, tell me what this "showdown" involves and I will determine if I am going to participate in it or simply kill you all."

Mark nodded, "The showdown is as follows. You bring the stolen nuclear weapon here. That is what you will forfeit if you lose. When it is here, in play so to speak, then you and I will compete in a challenge of physical combat. If I defeat you, then we are declared the winners and we will be allowed to take the stolen weapon back to our world. If, on the other hand, you defeat me, then my life is forfeit as are my friends here and you are declared the winner. Any and all weapons are permitted and cheating will be overlooked."

Satan stood there for a while contemplating the challenge and the possibilities. "I am stronger and more formidable than you are. I have millions of demons and you can't call on God or angelic forces. You have overestimated yourself and underestimated me, again. I accept your challenge."

A large device appeared behind Satan. "All right, here is the stolen weapon. Shall we begin?"

Mark smiled, "Not so fast. I have a right to examine the device to assure that it truly is the stolen property before we begin combat."

Satan smiled an evil smile and motioned Mark to look the device over. He stalked back to where the other demons stood waiting to attack.

Mark walked over to the bomb and checked it over. He ensured it was the stolen Israeli weapon, serial number and all. He nodded and walked back to the other two warriors. Turning around he said, "To start off the festivities I will tell you that I too, have a nuclear weapon here." He indicated the Mule behind him. You can check it out if you don't believe me. If I feel I am going to lose to you or your demons, I will detonate it immediately which will eliminate us, the demons within twenty miles and your entire domain in the same distance. Shall we begin?"

The devil shook his head, "That was not in the agreement."

Mark smiled, 'Oh, yes it was. I said, "any and all weapons were permitted. And you agreed to that."

The devil also smiled and said, "Then we need to kill you before you can use your toy." All of the demons surrounding the team rushed forward to kill them at one time.

Mark said, "Guys, the new body armor includes functioning Force Generators so have fun eliminating demons."

The biggest and fastest demons reached the three warriors and swung their swords, grabbed with their claws, bit with their fangs, and anything else they had to attack the humans with. Nothing touched the warriors who began cleaning out Satan's hordes with a vengeance.

Satan himself appeared next to Mark and swung a powerful stroke with his huge black sword only to see it bounce off Mark without any effect. He immediately willed himself back to the rear of the attacking demons to try to understand this new development.

In a split second he came before God in Heaven and decried the use of the technology against him and his forces. "Didn't you tell them that they couldn't use their "Force Generators?" You are cheating!"

The voice of God rolled over Satan. "They are not using their Force Generators. All of their units are under lock and key at their base in the world. I am not cheating. Now return to your place." In the wink of an eye Satan found himself back in the central caverns and no better off than before. His demons had realized that they couldn't hurt the humans and had run away to survive. Mark was walking up toward Satan with his accursed sword of God's power which Satan knew he couldn't stand up to. He put a field of force of his own up between him and Mark.

"You think you have won, but I can still show you that I am more powerful than you." He made a motion with his hand and the stolen nuclear weapon disappeared and Satan laughed and told Mark

I will destroy the accursed Holy City of Jerusalem and it will be a fate worse than death for the Israelis. Ha, Ha!" And he disappeared himself.

Mark kneeled down and praised Yahveh and Yahshua and thanked them for the victory. Suddenly they were back in the Armory of the Sea Base. Mark made sure the nuclear weapon was deactivated and not subject to spiritual manipulation or skull drudgery.

The three warriors turned off their body armor Force Generators and Jack looked at Mark. "How do you feel that we won and that any of this was worthwhile? Satan still has the stolen weapon and will detonate it at the Dome of the Rock. How did we win?"

Mark smiled and took a complex computer chip out of his shirt pocket. "Old Nick is going to have a hard time setting off that weapon without the command and control chip. When he tries to detonate it all that will happen is that the entire weapon will deactivate, melt, and become unusable. The U235 will degrade within a few hours and become inert. It is all part of the Israeli design to prevent their weapons from being reverse engineered or used without this chip. I was counting on Satan and his big ego to allow me to inspect the weapon while he was there watching me. He doesn't have a clue about that technology and never noticed that the self-destruct indicator lit up when I pulled the chip out. He will realize his mistake soon and he is going to seek revenge for sure."

Jack put his hand on his new body armor and asked Mark, "and how did you get this and why did it work when God told us we couldn't use them?"

Mark shrugged, "The day I was gone, I went to Denver on the "Myth" and the good Doctor Clashire at your plant had four of these new models available for me. You see, I realized when you said that God wouldn't let Satan win over his kids that He had given us a loophole in His agreement with old thermal britches. He said, *"I cannot allow you to use the Force Generators you have either."*

I realized that allowed us to use any Force Generators we didn't already "have".

Sarah shook her head, "Okay, how did you figure out that Satan would back down when you said you had a nuclear weapon that would fry twenty miles of his domain? How did you know that you could even kill demons with a weapon like that?"

CHAPTER THIRTY-EIGHT

Mark smiled at Sarah. "Honey, you overestimate the devil and, in this case, you underestimated me. Let me explain what happened here. It was mostly sleight of hand, misdirection, and sheer human gall."

"First, have you ever considered the fact that demons are fallen angels and therefore created beings?"

Sarah nodded her head. Mark continued, "If that is so, then how can we "kill" them with our swords?"

Sarah thought for a second. "We don't "kill" the spirit we kill the created being, right?"

Mark smiled, "That is true, but what happens to the demon when we destroy its created being?"

Sarah frowned, "I don't know. I assumed that the remaining spirit component of the created being goes to the pit until it is judged at the end of time."

Mark nodded again. "But I had always assumed that Satan used the created being element of a demon to make a physical body that could interface or fight with humanity in our physical dimension and that when we killed the physical body we were destroying the created being component. It turns out that it is a bit more complicated than that. When a demon is allowed by God to enter the human dimension it is still a demonic spirit without a physical component. It can't materialize here because there is no physical body to materialize."

"Because Satan has no creative ability he has to use an existing physical entity to house the demon. I don't know where he gets the ones he uses but once he fuses the "created being" element into the physical host it is permanent. God allows the demon with the physical body into the human dimension and we use our swords to kill the physically present demon, both the body and the created being are destroyed in all dimensions. The reason we can kill that combination is because our swords have the essence of Yahveh on them and it destroys both at once."

139

"Their physical host body doesn't really exist in our dimension. That is why, when we kill them with our swords their bodies dissipate as smoke or fumes. When the created being component of the demon is destroyed there is no energy left to maintain the physical body."

"Also, when their created being is destroyed the spirit component has no place to go except to the pit to await judgment."

Mark continued, "As you know, if Satan gives a demon a body and doesn't get God's approval to allow entry into our dimension and he transports them here anyway, they don't have their spiritual characteristics such as immunity to bombs and bullets. If we kill the illegal entry, it also goes to the pit after it is killed."

"Now, consider what happens when the created being component of a demon is destroyed when it is in the demonic realm. Nothing different than if it is killed here. The spirit can roam and look for a "being" it can appropriate for its own. If there are none available, then it ends up in the pit awaiting judgment. Remember the portion of the demonic realm or dimension we destroyed with the small nuclear weapon when God told us to leave nothing of that portion of the demonic realm standing?"

Sarah shivered as she remembered that fun trip. She nodded her head. "Yes, I remember it well. We had killed all of the demons there before we set off the bomb and God translated us back here."

Mark nodded, "Yes, he did. But, remember what the Archangel Raquel told us after that battle in the demonic realm: *He (Satan) was far enough away, but he sacrificed over six thousand demons in the blast.* "So, if a 50 pound, tactical field nuke could kill six thousand demons in the demonic realm, how many could a one-megaton nuclear bomb destroy and send to the pit?"

That meant we were able to hurt Satan greatly if we could get that large of a weapon into the demonic realm. God couldn't translate us and the bomb there, so we had to trick Satan into doing that, which my "challenge" did just that. You see, he just isn't that smart."

CHAPTER THIRTY-NINE

Jack and Mark returned the borrowed nuke and explained the elimination of the stolen nuke to General Levy. As they returned to the Sea Base Jack looked at Mark. "I have to congratulate you on about six slick things that derailed a really nasty situation for Israel and the Temple Mount. But, something has been chewing on me since we returned. Doesn't everything that happened seem to have been too easy, too quick, and too much of a slam dunk against the greatest evil on the planet. I know you are good and so are the rest of the Team but, really?"

Mark sat there frowning. "Sadly, I agree with you. I thought it was a brilliant coup we pulled off on Satan, but in retrospect, I believe you're right. It seemed like a mountain but in truth, it didn't turn out to be much more than a bump in the road. Considering the power and intensity of the conflict involving a major character like Satan and based on life as I've seen it, something was definitely missing from such a serious encounter. Usually, what comes next is really, really bad. We absolutely need to get the Core Team together again to pray and seek God for what we missed and what we need to do right now."

Calling the Core Team together they explained what they now thought about the showdown with Satan. Then Jack explained, "God couldn't give us guidance due to whatever agreement He had made with Satan. We should be able to seek His wisdom now and find out what we need to prepare for or do immediately."

Jack led the Team in prayer and after they had praised and worshiped Yahveh in Yahshua's name they sought wisdom and guidance.

As they fell silent Jack sensed brightness through his closed eyes and opened them to behold the angels Rose, Caleb, and Hugo standing among them.

Jack smiled, "Hello warriors of God. Have you come to enlighten us concerning our prayers?"

Rose and Caleb deferred to Hugo who answered. "Yes, the Most High has honored us to "enlighten" you and your team as to the recent events and the future."Hugo sat down on, nothing. "As one of your fictional detectives once said, "There is foulness afoot" and for a very good reason. I think that applies in this situation."

"First, let me summarize your recent confrontation with the demon of darkness. You were right about the theft of the nuclear weapon It was a trick to lure you and the other team members into a confrontation that would either set you up be blamed for destruction of the Temple Mount or kill you. Your "challenge" changed Satan's plans somewhat. He decided to go along with the challenge to test the waters and possibly eliminate you."

"His inability to destroy you, Sarah, or Jack caused him to run to God to complain about the Force Generators. God explained your correctness as to His conditions, rebuked him and sent him back to face you. You were right that the Most High left you an out by limiting the Force Generators you couldn't use to those you already had. When Satan returned he knew he couldn't defeat you with the Force Generator and your anointed sword and was afraid that you would destroy him. So, he thought he would take the stolen weapon and detonate it on the Temple Mount and leave you with nothing but guilt for allowing him escape and use the weapon on Jerusalem."

Hugo smiled, "I think your investigation of his bomb, which caused the weapon to not detonate but actually become useless instead, right at his moment of victory, may have actually caused the devil more intensive anger than ever before in history. He acted very strange for quite a while after that and killed scores of his own demons."

"Now, as to the coming events which Satan has been planning for your team. Mark, your recent "showdown" has caused him to change his plans considerably by making yourself his greatest nemesis. His original plan was to turn the Jewish Mossad against your Team by blaming the assassination of the Director of the Mossad on the Crossfire Team. That plan was thwarted by Jack's previous and new association with the new Director of the Mossad. Satan then planned to have the Mossad blame your group for stealing and detonating the Israeli nuclear weapon on the Temple Mount."

"With that failure, we believe he has decided to put all his many plans on hold and concentrate all of his demons and his demonic efforts to destroying your team. This decision of Satan's has always been the Most High's plan for this time."

Hugo looked with sympathy at the stricken looks on the faces of the Team members. Then he smiled, "But, be of good cheer. True, Satan's focus has been totally focused on you through his defeats by the Team, and especially by Mark, but that is what God has desired for this present time. By focusing on you, he is ignoring and letting slip many other plans, machinations, and evil works he had designed to destroy much of the humanity that the Most High still wants to save."

Jack looked at Hugo with concern. "I can understand why God would want to save as much of the unsaved before the return of His Son but, if Satan brings the entire force of his evil empire against the forty-five people of the Crossfire Team, how will we remain alive on Earth to serve Him until the midpoint of the tribulations?"

Hugo nodded his head. "That is an insightful question. The Most High created this threat to shape the activities of Satan in these end times."

Caleb made a motion with his right hand and everyone in the Sensitive Operations Group of the Crossfire Team appeared standing in ranks behind the Core Team.

Hugo solemnly stated, "Now, hear the word of Yahveh."

"My children, you have been faithful and you are very special to me. I have used your abilities and faithfulness to direct Satan's anger and rage away from the poor and defenseless and against your team. Many battles face all of you because of this. Therefore, I and my messengers will fight with you against the enemy. Remember, the enemy will use temptations, threats, trickery, and war against each and all of you. Stand rock solid against everything the evil realm does, and I will stand with you to defend you and encourage you. You will be victorious in My Name over everything evil."

Rose held out her hands and a golden anointing spread from her hands to all of the people in the room.

Laura felt so loved and refreshed as the beautiful anointing fell on her. Her faith and strength suddenly knew no bounds and a vision of Heaven appeared before her. She knew she would stand for Yahveh and Yahshua against the hordes of hell and win. Her determination was unending.

As the anointing ended Hugo raised his hands and said, "Rest in the Most High and remember we will also be with you." The three angels disappeared.

Jack was still humbled, thrilled, and ready. The members of the Team who had not been there originally faded out of sight and Jack said, "All praise and glory to Yahveh God the Father." Everyone else echoed that truth.

CHAPTER FORTY

The Core Team resumed their seats in the War Room quietly and waited for Jack to speak.

Jack continued to pray for guidance as to their next steps. He suddenly had a complex battle plan laid out before him in his mind. He studied the plan and sat up in his seat. "Okay, based on what the Father is telling me, we need to become the gorillas in our battles with Satan and his demons. The best defense is a good offense. We need to strike the enemy where we can do the most harm and keep them off balance and worried about what we are going to do rather than the other way around.

Mark spoke up, "Why don't we find out if there is a way we can know when the demonic attack teams are going to leave their dimension and when and where. Then we battle them until the more intelligent of the attackers see that they are losing and they flee back into their dimension. Maybe we can attach a small but potent explosive to the fleeing ones so that when they return to the demonic realm they blow up a bunch of their fellow demons as well as their selves."

Jack smiled, "I like it but it would be tricky to plant bombs on them wouldn't it?"

Mark laughed, "Normally, yes. But, if one had a Force Generator in special mode it could be done."

Laura added, "Okay, but wouldn't their demon leaders figure out what is happening and prevent the demons from returning to their dimension or the demon decides to become a suicide bomber on our side?"

Mark nodded, "If we set them up only to detonate in the demonic realm they would just become inert and could be retrieved and used again."

"What if we could find a way to fire a small missile into the demonic realm when their demons are entering our dimension?" Alexis asked.

Jack looked at Charlie. "What do you think?"

Charlie shrugged his shoulders. "How do we know that the portal the demons use to enter our dimension isn't a one-way portal? We need more information on this transfer mechanism."

Jack spoke into the air. "Raquel, can you assist us?"

The Archangel Raquel appeared next to Jack. "I'll do what I can to help you."

Jack outlined their questions. Raquel thought for a few seconds. "Hugo".

Hugo appeared and Raquel spoke in a heavenly language that only took twelve words to cover the problems raised. Hugo conferred in an unknown medium with an unknown entity. He then looked at Jack and spoke in English. "An audacious plan to say the least. I can show Carol how to interpret the Matrix as to when and where there will be an entrance between the dimensions. Then you can send your missiles through the dimensional portal but it must be done exactly at the same time that a demon is passing through it the other direction. Your people with the missiles must know the amount of time it takes a missile to be fired and transition the distance to the portal so that it is there at the right time."

"Forget the idea of placing a bomb on a retreating demon. Satan will catch onto that quickly and simply block the portals so that there is no escape for demons once they are in our dimension. Their lives are meaningless to him."

Mark nodded his head. "Okay for phase one. I've got to do some thinking for phase two. Please, Hugo, train Carol to interpret the Matrix so that she can give us adequate time to be ready when the enemy comes through the portal."

Hugo laughed, "Don't worry about that. They have to generate a high level of energy at the position of the dimensional gap for at least fifteen of your minutes before they can establish a reliable connection to pass through."

Jack frowned, "But, what if Satan doesn't list the demons on the Matrix but just sends them through where and when he wants to?"

Hugo smiled, "Remember, Satan has lost his right to use the eleventh dimension. So, he can't do that anymore."

The two angels disappeared.

Jack pointed at Mark and Charlie. "Make it work."

Laura called Carol Moffet and started to explain what they would need when Carol stopped her. "Hugo already explained what we need to do and spent three days with me at the Matrix showing me how to determine time and place for the dimensional shifts of all demons. I'm ready."

CHAPTER FORTY-ONE

Mark worked with the Mossad and the IDF to acquire a large quantity of shoulder-fired missiles and launchers very quickly. The IDF had a great number of these launchers and missiles that they had confiscated from terrorist groups in the area. The IDF was glad to let the Crossfire Team use them against demons.

Mark, Sarah, David, and Alexis trained twenty of the SOG forces on how to use the launchers and the accuracy and timing required to get the missiles to enter the demonic realm.

Two days after the decision was made, the troops were ready for battle.

Mark called Jack and asked him to meet at the Armory. When jack showed up Mark walked up to him and showed him one of the four new body armors with the built-in Force Generator. Mark pushed the switch and the green LED lit up brightly. Mark grinned, "I think the Father sees this all-out attack as a distinct advantage for the dark powers and is allowing us to use the FGs to offset that advantage."

Jack whistled. "That's a game changer for sure. Let's check the earlier Generators and make sure they work also."

Mark smiled again, "I already checked them; they operate just like these. Let's issue them to all the members of the Team and take the war to Satan every chance we get."

Jack's battle com chimed and he answered it. Carol was on the line. "Jack, there are forty demons scheduled to drop into the flight line between us and the Mossad base in twenty minutes. It seems the angelic coverage is for our Sea Base portion and not the Mossad's area or the area in between."

Jack thanked her and activated the all member's alarm. "Troops, there will be a forty demon attack at our air field in the next fifteen minutes. All hands respond now."

Mark looked concerned, "What if they just open up a riff rather than come through individually?"

Jack's eyes had turned to green ice. "Then we send twenty missiles into the demonic dimension at one time!"

Jack grabbed the two extra new version body armor Generators and handed one to Mark. "Give that to Sarah, we'll have to give the other Generators after this attack. It'll be up to the four of us to defend the rest. Both men ran for their apartments to give their wives the armor.

Everyone assembled on the air field where Carol pointed out the invasion point. Jack explained the new arrangements for the FGs and told everyone after firing the missiles, to drop back and use their rifles. Mark, Sarah, Laura, and he would stand forth to battle since they were protected.

Megan Cole and Alexis offered to fight the demons without the Generators, but Jack vetoed that thought. "We've only got a few minutes and no time to try and get the other Force Generators. Use your rifles and see if any of the demons are here illegally."

Twenty SOG members knelt or stood with their shoulder-mounted missiles ready when there was a series of crackling, ripping, and popping sounds as forty demons started stepping out of their dimension into the human dimension near the airfield.

Twenty missiles were fired and eighteen of them entered single-demon riffs and created mass destruction somewhere in the demonic dimension. The other two missiles killed eight of the demons that had just entered our dimension. Twenty-five rifles fired almost as one and fifteen of the remaining thirty-two demons were killed as the rounds tore big holes through them. Another eight demons died from a second round of rifle fire. The nine, legal demons, headed for the team members and were met by Jack, Laura, Mark, and Sarah in their armor and swords.

The battle was brief because of the Force Generators. The four Crossfire Warriors waded into the nine demons without worrying about damage and dispatched the demons quickly. Jack used his battle-COMM and warned the others that there might be a second wave.

But, after thirty minutes there were no more attacks and Carol told Jack that three more Sea Base attacks that had been scheduled were suddenly cancelled from the schedule on the Matrix.

Retiring to the base, Mark asked Jack, "Why don't we ask Raquel to expand the angelic protection to the entire Sea Base?"

Jack shrugged."We can try that, but I would expect that the angels would have already done that, if it were possible."

After they filed their reports and cleaned their equipment, the two men met with the Archangel Raquel.

Mark explained the problem to Raquel and the angel shook his head. "Unfortunately, the Most High ordered us to only protect the Crossfire Team. He can't have us defend the Mossad portion of the base because; there are people over there that could be used by the enemy against both us and your team if we provided coverage for the entire base. Your team has been seasoned, cleansed, and is totally dedicated to serving Yahshua and the Most High. Many of their people do not accept Yahshua. To assure your protection we would probably have to destroy some of the personnel on the Mossad side and that would not be appreciated and the Most High will not allow it anyway."

Mark shook his head sadly. "I am sorry for them." He realized something and asked, "Raquel, if the enemy can compromise some of the people on the Mossad side of the base, why don't they do that?"

Raquel thought for a few seconds. "It's complicated, but, many of the personnel on the Mossad portion of the base are dedicated Jews who serve the Most High and that arrangement pre-dates Yahshua's time on Earth. It is a completely different covenant that the Most High honors differently than His covenant with you. It is most comprehensive and is efficient at preventing most demonic attack or influence."

Two weeks later there still had not been any additional mass attacks on the Sea Base. The consensus was that Satan had learned a lesson from the missile attack and decided not to do any more of those, for now.

CHAPTER FORTY-TWO

At least twice a week, Jack took time to stop and see his Mom and Dad and his Uncle Larry and his wife, Gavina. Gavina was of Spanish descent and had been out of the U.S. when the others had accepted a ride in the "Ghost" (then called the X-76). After returning to the Sea Base, Jack had sent David and Alexis to Mexico to accompany her to their base in Israel. She was an assistant to Pastor Larry, her husband, and specialized in south-of-the-border cooking and was exceptionally good at it.

Jack had been surprised to learn that both his folks and his aunt and uncle had also had a visit from an angel who had explained that they could have gone in the Rapture or they could remain on Earth until the mid-point of the seven-year Tribulation period to serve Yahveh and Yahshua. All four of them had agreed to stay and fight for the Lord although they had not been aware that they were destined to join the Crossfire Team in Israel.

Jack's Uncle Larry had been a Pastor of a small church in Texas and had spent twenty years in the U.S. Air Force in his younger years. He recognized that at his age of 79 that he and the other three "senior" member's fighting days were behind them. But, he was intrigued by why Jesus would have directly intervened in their lives. They had found a Messianic Synagogue and had attended Sabbath and Shabbat services in Tel Aviv until the recent all-out war between Satan and the Crossfire Team. Now, for their safety they attended the Team's own Synagogue inside the Crossfire Base.

Jack and Laura decided to spend some time with them this morning and located them in the large forested area to the South of the air field and the entrance to the Team's base.

They were having a picnic to celebrate the American holiday of the 4th of July. Gavina had spent most of the previous day cooking for the event. They were in high spirits and had just started the meal when the Malones showed up.

Steve waved at the two family members as they walked up. "Hey guys, welcome. Grab a chair and join us. Gavina has made enough food for everyone."

Jack and Laura sat down and were served a heaping plate of tamales, tostadas, and other Mexican dishes along with iced tea.

Larry had questions and engaged them in a hearty discussion that everybody joined in. The conversation turned humorous and lasted for almost an hour.

Without warning six demons appeared out of a riff that formed suddenly near the group. These were the slick types with slim black blades and more or less human appearance. Two of the demons grabbed Gavina and Steve and held them with a sword to their throats. One of the demons looked at Jack and Laura. In a surprisingly deep and guttural voice the apparent lead demon spoke to Jack. "You will come with us or we will kill these two people."

Jack stood up and Laura followed suit. Jack's eyes had turned a cold, icy green. He simply said, "Let them go now or we will destroy all of you and I promise you we will also destroy a large portion of your demonic realm."

Larry stood up and advanced on the demons holding his wife and his brother. "In the name and the blood of Jesus I command you to release these people and return to your world. Father God, I ask your warrior angels to remove these detestable creatures and protect my wife and my brother."

The two demons holding the hostages started shaking and released both people. Steve took Gavina's hand and led her back to the table. The two demons that had held them suddenly disappeared in a lightning flash of white power.

The leader of the demons advanced on Larry who simply stared at him as it raised its sword. There was another flash and the angels Rose and Caleb appeared between the demon and the Pastor.

The demon back peddled and raised his sword to combat the angels. The other six demons rushed toward the angels with their swords swinging in anger.

Jack and Laura urgently started praying as they ran toward the demons and their armor and swords exploded into sight. Jack used his COMM-link to Mark and asked for help to protect his relatives.

Seeing the gold and silver warriors rushing at them caused the eight remaining demons to veer away from the angels to battle the human warriors. The two forces came together with a terrific crash. Jack ran one of the demons through as they struck each other.

Laura in her golden armor went into high speed time management and cut down two of the demons and turned back to the others. Three of the demons came at Jack at one time while the other two went after Laura. All at once Caleb appeared between Jack and Laura and destroyed two of the demons attacking Jack.

Rose appeared behind the leader of the demons and ran it through while it rose up to strike Larry. Suddenly eight more demons ran out of the riff and attacked the two human and two angelic warriors.

All eight of the demons were struck in the head by a flurry of rifle rounds and all eight were destroyed as big holes obliterated their heads. All at once Mark, Sarah, David, Alexis, and Carol rushed up to the picnic area and engaged the remaining demons.

Larry was praying for the humans and the angels and Steve, Gavina, and Donna joined him in prayer and were calling down the fire of Yahveh against the demons as the battle swirled around them.

Ethan Reaper and Elon ran around the battle and dropped to their knees. Each one raised a shoulder mounted missile launcher and together they fired two Stinger missiles directly into the riff. As the huge explosions shattered the demonic area inside the riff it flickered twice and snapped shut with a loud bang. Both men dropped their launchers and started praying. Their armor and swords appeared and they ran toward the waning battle. Before they got there the last of the demons were destroyed and everyone's armor and swords disappeared.

Jack checked his relatives and the rest of the Team members for damage but there was none. He looked at the two angels and saw that they were also unhurt. He thanked them both for their efforts on his elder's behalf and the support the Team had received.

Caleb winked at him and disappeared. Rose drifted over to the four older people and stopped in front of Larry. "You exhibited great faith in the face of sure death. Since you were willing to lay down your life for your friends, Yahshua sees your faith in Him as great on Earth and in Heaven." She held out her right hand and a cloud of sparkling motes flowed from her hand and covered Larry. She smiled at all the people. "Yahshua's peace be with you all." She swirled into a rush of gold and white and faded from sight.

Jack walked over to his Uncle and put his arm around Larry's shoulders. "Thank you for your bravery on our behalf. I love you all." Jack smiled at Gavina, Donna, and Steve.

Mark came over and shook all four of the elder's hands. "I think from now on you will probably have to have your picnics in the park in the atrium inside our part of the base where the angels keep the demons from entering."

Laura also came over and hugged each of the older people. "I will see that we have the atrium altered to give you the same peaceful area like this one, without the demons of course."

Jack waved all of the Team members to gather around. "First, I want to commend each and every one of you for your quick reaction and efforts in this matter. I am going to have Gavina organize several of us to help her and we are going to make for a bigger Fourth of July celebration in the atrium for all of the Team and our elders in three days."

Gavina nodded her head, "That is a great idea, but I won't need any help cooking, really."

Laura asked, "Are you sure? You're talking about fifty to sixty people."

Gavina grinned, "I've done church fellowship meals with over a hundred by myself. Anyway, that way I don't have to train anyone else; I just get it done."

On advice from Larry, backed up by Steve, Jack decided it would be prudent to allow Gavina do it her way. He told Laura to oversee the rest of the celebration and coordinate the food with Gavina. Laura just smiled and nodded.

Steve came over and asked Jack and Laura to make the party a special one because it would also be celebrating Larry's recently passed eightieth birthday.

Jack said, "I'll see what we can arrange."

CHAPTER FORTY-THREE

The next morning at 6:00 A.M., Jack called a breakfast staff meeting of the three primary couples of the Crossfire Team. He wanted to brainstorm the current situation and get their opinions and the possible options.

Six thousand, eight hundred, and fifty miles west of Tel Aviv, in Denver Colorado, USA, it was 9:00 P.M. the previous evening. Christi Steele was so excited as she sat watching her best friend Rachel Reynolds as she was up on stage starring in a pre-screening of an Indie movie of a play she had starred in two years before. This film had been submitted and accepted to be shown at the Sundance Film Festival.

Rachel and Christi had suffered through their teenage years together as they completed high school as best friends and confidents. They had supported each other as one or the other met the "perfect "guy" and eventually fell out of love and "got over" the relationships, several times. Then they each went to a different local college but maintained their friendship through it all. Rachel evolved into a slim beauty with good acting skills and a photogenic élan that made her "desirable" for acting jobs. Her dark hair and intense brown eyes hid a generous heart and a spirit committed to Jesus, her Savior.

Christi was proud of "Rache" and her acting talents. She had actually seen a slightly earlier cut of the film and was attempting to watch the final cut of the film carefully. But, she was distracted by three events that had happened in her life recently. She had three dreams in the last two weeks that kept returning to her mind.

The first dream she saw an angel. Not just any angel, but a beautiful angel named Rose. When she was overseas over two years ago she had met this angel as she was attempting to escape from Zyngola with her step-sister-in-law, Laura Malone and a former Mossad Agent and Assassin named Sarah Connelly. They had quite an adventure and Christi had seen Laura change into a golden warrior with a

156

sword that flowed with the Glory or Esteem of Yahveh. Laura had taken on a huge ugly demon and defeated it.

Christi knew she'd never forget that time. But, she was surprised when she found the angel Rose in her dreams. Her mind wandered away from the film as she thought about the dream. She had found herself in a beautiful and modern garden. She had been standing on a large and lovely grassy area near a huge mansion which she saw but couldn't recall any details about it.

Rose had suddenly appeared and drew close to Christi in the dream. Rose studied Christi and then spoke to her. "Christi, the Most High asked me to bring you greetings. I have come to prepare you for a stressful time in the near future. The enemy of all mankind has declared an all-out war against the Crossfire Team and is looking for any way to attack or bring pressure against the team. Satan is aware of your relationship with Jack Malone and is seeking to harm or kill you to hurt him. Be aware and stay strong in your faith. You were not selected to be called to Heaven in the Rapture, but that was not because you were unworthy. You have an important role to play in the future of the Crossfire Team in the near future."

"You will be called to Heaven at the mid-point of the Tribulations but you have a critical mission for Yahveh until then. I will help prepare you and defend you until that time. I will speak to you again soon."

The angel and the dream faded out and Christi had come awake in the dark of her bedroom sitting up and with her eyes wide open. As she thought about the dream she realized that she was probably only dreaming what she wanted to have happen. She let the dream fade out of her mind and went back to sleep.

A week and a half later she had a second dream. This one was even stranger than the first. She found herself in the beautiful garden again and this time Rose appeared and spread her arms wide. A burst of energy, or light, or something, focused on Christi and she felt filled with power and force. This dream ended quickly. Now she wasn't too quick to write either dream off as self-adoration.

Two nights ago she had the third and definitely the most strenuous dream. Rose was there in the garden again and this dream lasted what seemed like days. Christi found herself dressed in golden armor that covered her completely from the top of her head to the soles of her feet. Only her face was unarmored. She also had a six-foot silver and chrome sword in her hands and she was filled with information and knowledge on how to use it properly. She went through hundreds of exercises and techniques in the dream and then woke up as it faded.

In the darkness of her room she sat in her bed and noticed changes in the carriage of her body, her arms and hands. Even her legs felt strange. She turned on the light and stood before her full length mirror. She felt much stronger all over but her arms were positively like steel. Now, she was seriously confused.

She got down on her knees and prayed that God would tell her what was going on with the dreams. She didn't get an answer but she was filled with a great peace that thrilled her in its sweetness. She shook her head slightly and turned back to the film. Rachel hadn't noticed her wool-gathering as she watched the film. Christi hadn't told her best friend about her dreams either.

After the showing, they walked to a small café they both liked. They had a light supper and decided to walk home because it was only ten or twelve blocks from the café. Plus, it would save them the cab fares.

Six blocks from her apartment, where Rachel's car was parked, they ran into trouble. Twelve members of a gang were sitting in front of an old home drinking. When they saw the two women and especially the attractiveness of Christi with her full figure, blonde hair, and pretty face, the gang decided to induct both women into their gang, but first, they would both have to please all of the men.

Rachel pulled out her cell phone to call 9-1-1 but the leader of the gang pulled out a handgun and smiled and shook his head.

Rachel knew she wasn't going to be any problem for the heavily muscled gang members who exhibited vicious attitudes and looked to have no scruples about hurting her.

To prevent the two women from getting away, several of the gang members ran through the front yards and stepped out onto the sidewalk behind the thoroughly frightened women.

Christi looked up and down the street, but there was no traffic at this hour on the normally busy street. There didn't seem to be any hope of rescue. She wanted to despair but the anger building inside her wouldn't let her do it.

Just as the three groups of people came together on the sidewalk Christi saw the shadowy outline in the dark of the largest member of the gang coming up behind the main group of men in front of her and Rachel.

Christi's eyes grew large as she saw the new, dimly seen member slap several of the gang members away with an unnatural power and then wade into the main group.

Suddenly aware of the problem behind them, most of the gang turned and pulled out handguns. They started shooting at the intruder. Then a car turned onto the street from a side street and the headlights illuminated the battle.

CHAPTER FORTY-FOUR

Christi's insides froze as she realized that the newcomer was a physically present demon and not human at all. Ugly, gross, smelly, and very violent it was using a large black sword and hacking the gang members to death with big swings of the blade. The gunfire from the gang members did not seem to affect the demon at all.

The acrid smell of the demon, blood, and gun powder gagged both her and Rachel as the gang was quickly whittled down. Christi looked behind her but the gang members there had run away after seeing the true nature of the demon.

She wanted to run away too, but she knew the demon would catch them from behind and kill them both. She was fairly sure that the demon was there to kidnap or kill her.

As the demon ran its sword through the leader and used the blade to cast him aside, there was no one left but her and Rachel. To her credit, Rachel stepped forward in defiance of the demon regardless of her fear. Christi knew that in a few seconds, Rachel would be killed and then the demon would deal with her.

Christi was almost desolated by the inevitable death facing both of them. Then she heard a lovely voice in her mind, "Pray to God continuously!"

The demon stepped closer to the frightened women and raised its sword to cut them both in half.

Christi started praying and the set of golden armor covered her along with a golden shield exploding into sight lighting up the street. The awesome chrome sword she had handled in her dream appeared in her right hand with the Esteem of Yahveh flowing off of the blade in waves that made the demon weak and made it stop advancing.

Completely surprised, Christi stood there for a second uncertain what to do. Then, seeing the murder in the three eyes of the demon suddenly brought a solid series of steps to her understanding.

Acting decisively, she used her left hand to move Rachel behind her as her mind filled with attack and defense strategies. She stepped forward and acted like she was going to use a cross body stroke from her right to her left, which made the larger demon turn to its left and place its sword into a vertical blocking stroke to deflect her blade. Instead, Christi spun around to her right, on her left heel, and cut the demon in half at the waist from its unprotected side. The demon let out a deep bass bellow of agony. It dropped its sword and began to turn to smoke and demon stain which splattered on the sidewalk.

Christi stepped back, with her sword in high guard position as the demon and its black sword disappeared. Christi was very surprised that the combat had seemed completely natural to her.

She stopped praying in the spirit and her armor and sword vanished. As the area became dark again, Christi turned to see Rachel standing there with her mouth wide open and her body shaking with relief.

While Rachel tried to find her voice for a few seconds, Christi took that time to drop to one knee and thank God and give Him praise for everything that she had just done. She realized she was operating on a new pattern that had been implanted in her mind in her dreams. Still in amazement and awe she took a deep breath and recognized that she had become more than she was before. She also realized she had seen this before in Zyngola when Laura had done the same thing.

She got to her feet, reached out and took Rachel's arm and gently led her out into the street and away from the slaughter house scene and toward Christi's apartment. There still were no sirens, no shouts, just quiet.

Rachel finally got all her parts working as she stopped near her car. "Christi, what was that thing? And what did you do? And how did you know how to do that?"

Christi hugged her best friend and felt her pull back a little. She said softly, "It's alright Rache. That thing was a demon and I believe it was sent here to kill me. Apparently, my step-brother and his organization have irritated the demonic realm and they came here to eliminate me and thereby punish him. As for the golden armor and the sword, it is a gift from God to allow me to battle things like that. I know. I have seen Laura use the same armor before in Zyngola, Africa to kill another demon."

Rachel looked nervously left and right. "Are there any more demons around?"

Christi shook her head. "I don't know, but I doubt it." God dropped a word into her mind. "But, I am going to call my step-brother and his wife and see what I have become involved in. This whole thing is a God thing and I will have to go to Israel to get a full understanding. You stay strong and don't worry about demons. They most likely won't bother you as long as I'm not here, okay?"

Rachel was returning to her normal self. "No, it's not all right. I don't want you to leave." A thought appeared in her mind and she realized she was whining when this event was much more important than her needs. She also realized that Christi didn't ask for this and was caught up in things she couldn't control. "Who is going to share late night chocolate with me?"

Christi put a smile on her face. "Okay, I will call you as I can. Tell everybody that I had to go overseas to see some relatives. Don't mention what just happened and act surprised if you hear about it." She stepped closer to her and placed her right hand on Rachel's left shoulder. "Rachel, be filled with the peace of Jesus over all this."

Rachel sighed as she watched Christi leave and walk determinedly toward her apartment building. For her, everything this night was new, scary, exciting, and horrible and terrifying but the thing that stunned her and that made the biggest impression on her was the complete peace that had filled her mind, body, and her soul when Christi had placed her hand on her shoulder and spoke peace over her.

As Christi reached the door she turned and waved to Rachel and then went into her apartment. She thought that she should be shaken up by the events of tonight but instead she was galvanized with a solid determination to accomplish her short term goals and find out what this "mission" from God was all about. This was definitely a "new" her. She picked up her cell phone.

CHAPTER FORTY-FIVE

The staff meeting was just finishing when Jack got a phone call. He answered it to hear his step-sister, Christi, calling from Denver. He listened to her for a full five minutes and said, "Okay, be careful and we'll see you tomorrow." Jack hung up and called all the people there back into the room.

"Guys, I just had an interesting call from my step-sister Christi Steele in Denver." He saw interest on everyone's faces. "It seems our war with Satan is getting wider. Two hours ago on a dark street, Christi and her friend Rachel were walking home from a movie and they were attacked by a demon." Jack immediately saw the fear and concern on Laura and Sarah's faces.

"They are all right. It seems that the angel Rose has been busy. Christi started praying and was given a set of armor and a sword like ours. I would have said before that she wouldn't have a clue as to what to do with a sword, but she battled the demon and destroyed it. She mentioned an intensive dream of training in sword combat and it all came back to her as she faced the demon. She is coming here to get a better understanding of a "mission" she says Rose told her she had for Yahveh in another dream. And, she said that Rose told her she had an important role to play in the Crossfire Team."

Sarah smiled, "Another sister in arms."

Jack nodded, "I am surprised and gratified that our Father gave her the tools to defend herself, but curious as to why it was allowed to go that way rather than just having Rose defeat the demon for her and her friend. There is more to this new "sister-in-arms" than just being trained so that she could defend herself. I sense that there may be more to Christi's "mission" than she knows. Let's pray and be prepared when she gets here tomorrow."

He looked at Laura, "Would you please arrange a ticket for her from Denver to Tel Aviv and arrange for someone to meet her at Ben Gurion Airport?"

Sarah broke in as she shook her head. "No can do. The current administration in Washington has placed a moratorium on travel to Israel due to their conflicting position on the Anti-Christ Marco Marino."

Jack looked at Sarah and nodded. "I'll arrange a trip in either the Ghost or the Myth and I want you two and possibly Megan to go get her. Mark and I have a conference later today with General Levy. Now, this will be a very fast trip and starts right now. I'll get Christi to drive to a remote place in Wyoming to avoid contention with the Military around Denver."

Laura and Sarah headed for their apartments to get whatever they needed for the "fast trip" as Jack called the R&D headquarters on the Sea Base to request a plane. Mark figured the times and pointed out a remote area in Southern Wyoming that would serve their needs. Jack got the times from Mark and the location in the state above Colorado. Then he called Christi back.

As Laura, Sarah, and Megan were headed to the R&D hanger they were joined by Su Li. Laura asked, "Hello to you, young lady. Are you joining us for this trip?"

Su Li nodded her head. "Yes, I convinced Jack you needed a pilot too. Even though these planes are autonomous you never know." Su Li looked at Sarah with a smile. "Especially, after I read about your landing in Zyngola."

The four women were given the Myth as their vehicle and quickly boarded. The door sealed and the view screen at the front came to life with a wide angle view of the world in front of the aircraft. At present it showed the massive hanger door opening. The plane silently left the hanger and worked its way onto the runway, through the flight corridor and out from under the island off of the sea coast of Israel.

The flight was uneventful and extremely quick. Six thousand miles doesn't take long when you are traveling at Mach 6 or 4,102.2 miles per hour. An hour and a half after takeoff the Myth settled to the ground near a single car parked in a remote parking area off of Interstate 25 in Wyoming, south of the city of Cheyenne. They had loitered above the area until they were free of traffic to pick up Christi.

Everyone got out of the aircraft to meet Christi.

Christi Steele had turned into a supple and graceful blonde haired woman in her late twenties with a body shape that reflected her exercise and diet control. She did have a sweet tooth that she had to control, sometimes with a vengeance. Her deep blue eyes were usually thoughtful and friendly.

They were getting her luggage out of the trunk of the rent-a-car when, without warning, the Myth closed its door and silently lifted off and quickly rose out of sight.

Laura looked at Sarah with concern. "I don't see any traffic coming in either direction. Why did it leave?"

Sarah shrugged her shoulders and pulled out her cell phone. She dialed the number of the R&D lab at the Sea Base. There was no connection available. Sarah frowned; she dialed 9-1-1. She still had no connection. She looked up and said, "Everyone back into the car, we have to leave now!"

There was no panic and everyone smoothly replaced Christi's luggage and started to get into the car when two F-22 Raptor fighters flew over their position only three hundred feet above them.

Sarah thought for a few seconds. "Everyone, get out of the car!"

Everyone got out and looked to the ex-Mossad Agent for direction. "Apparently, the government is wise to us and is attempting to apprehend us. Pull your chips out of your cell phones and the break them. Throw all pieces of the phone away. They can use them to track us. Pray for Yahveh's assistance." Everyone started praying in their prayer languages. This was interrupted by the arrival of a large RV. The front door opened and a woman stepped out. "Are you ladies in trouble?" she asked.

Sarah nodded, "Our car broke down. Could you give us a lift to Cheyenne?"

The woman nodded her head. "Certainly, climb in." As she said this she pulled open the door to the living portion of the RV.

Christi opened the trunk and got her suitcase out. They all climbed into the RV. The lady shut the door and climbed into the driver's area and her husband drove out of the parking area and back onto the Interstate headed into the suburbs of the city of Cheyenne. Laura grinned at the others and casually pointed straight up.

Sarah was talking to Mrs. Gibson and her husband through the cut out from the living area. "We don't know how to thank you for the ride. It was lonely out there without a car."

Amy, as Mrs. Gibson turned out to be, laughed and agreed with Sarah. Mr. Gibson, or Abe, asked where they wanted to go in Cheyenne. Sarah said, "Any rent-a-car company so we can get another car."

Abe thought about that and nodded. "There is one about two miles ahead on our side of the road."

After they reached the rental company the team members got off and thanked Abe and Amy for the lift.

CHAPTER FORTY-SIX

Laura told the others to stay away from the office so as to not be recorded on the cameras she could see from outside. She went in and came out five minutes later with a contract and a set of keys. They walked to a large Chevrolet Tahoe and everyone got in. Laura drove off the lot and down the first main street she found. She found a closed store and pulled into the lot. She put the Tahoe in Park and turned around. "Let's quickly determine what is going on. I doubt that we have much time."

Sarah nodded, "We don't. We have had to make several changes just to stay free for a short time. It will not take the FBI long to determine how we got away from the car and then track us to this vehicle. We need to avoid confrontation with the FBI and drop completely off the grid. I think the pause we made on the Myth while waiting for the traffic to clear over the parking lot Christi's car was in, allowed the government to see the Myth and target the area. Either that or they were tracking Christi and we fell into the investigation. The first things we have to do is become invisible and stay away from the tens of thousands of cameras in this area. They will quickly find us when we gas this vehicle up and when we buy food."

Christi had been quiet up till then. "Why would they have been tracking me?"

Sarah grinned, "For one or more reasons. They could have somehow connected you to the dead bodies and demon stain from last night. They could have locked onto Jack's call to you or your call to him. They may know you are related to Jack. There are lots of possible reasons. That's not important right now. We need to reconnect to the Myth somehow and get out of the U.S. before we become permanent detainees, probably in Guantanamo."

Sarah said, "I wish we had a cell phone."

Christi spoke up. "I've still got mine and I have got a signal and connection. They must have your numbers but not mine, yet."

Sarah held out her hand and when she had Christi's phone she called the Mossad safe house in Dallas. She used the secret connection codes that ran through several cutouts and she got the agent in charge and told him that she was being hunted by the alphabet agencies in the U.S. and she needed to speak to Elon Lukin at the Crossfire Team Base. She told the agent she had retired from the Mossad but this would be important to the Mossad.

The agent told her to hold. Two minutes later Elon answered. Sarah asked to speak to Mark. Elon got Mark on the line in seconds. Sarah told Mark what was happening and asked what they needed to do.

Mark thought for a minute. "I've got an idea. First, can you avoid capture?"

Sarah sighed, "Possibly, they are very police state like here now. It will be through the favor of Yahveh that we are able to stay free. Contact the R&D department and find out why the Myth took off. This phone may be compromised soon. I love you." Sarah broke the connection and opened up Christi's phone. She took the chip out of it that allowed them to be tracked. She handed them both back to Christi. "Break that chip and throw them away, as soon as you can."

Laura said, "Let's go somewhere and ditch this vehicle and use our own good feet to get lost. We can go the opposite direction we want to go in and stop and get gas. Then farther and get food and camping supplies. Then we turn around and go where we can dump the SUV and find a way to get lost."

Sarah shook her head. "They know that one really well. Let's hide this beast, split up, and take a walk to places without cameras."

Christi was looking out the window. "I've got a better idea. Let's assume that this vehicle is low jacked. Why don't we act stupid and leave the keys in the ignition? Those two guys over there are almost drooling and they can't even see us."

Sarah looked at the two young thugs and grinned, "I like it. Grab Christi's luggage and let's act like we're going to check something out but leave the car running."

Everyone got out and left the SUV running as they walked around the corner like they were looking at the property. In less than two minutes they watched the SUV speed off down a side street. Su Li laughed, that should give the FBI something to chase for a while.

Splitting up into two groups, the women headed towards the edge of town and eventually found a large chain store and purchased some casual clothes, and makeup. Using the rest rooms, they changed clothes, hair, color, and hats. Christi left her luggage after rescuing her cosmetics, personal clothes, and jewelry. She put those things into a backpack she purchased.

They took the luggage out of the store and dropped it into a dumpster. It would be hard to spot them as the same women that had gone into the store.

Breaking into two groups again, they kept in sight of each other and headed away from Cheyenne and walked into the hills to the Southwest.

Finding a small, local used car lot that didn't look like it would have the internet let alone a security camera, Laura went in and found an eight-year-old Chevy Impala that had a lot of miles on it but sounded good and ran even better. Using cash, she always carried, she paid for the car and got a bill of sale and temporary plates.

She went a quarter mile and picked up the other four women and they headed even more to the South to make it harder to find them. They had been sailing along for almost forty minutes when they came over a hill and saw a road block a quarter mile away. Seeing a side road to the right Laura turned into it and wound around in the rural area for ten minutes when Su Li announced, "We've got company behind us.

A Wyoming County Sheriff's car was pulling up behind them with its red lights on. Laura pulled over and waited as the Deputy got out of his cruiser and came up to the driver's side of their car.

Laura lowered the power window and smiled at the officer. "Yes Sir, what is the problem?"

The officer was middle aged and somewhat gruff. "Your license and insurance card Ma'am"

Sarah knew this was going to be a problem because they didn't have any insurance as yet, probably never would either.

Laura dug out her old Colorado license and told the officer that they didn't have their insurance as yet but they were covered by their State Farm policy from their previous vehicle.

The officer looked at her license and went back to his cruiser to use his computer.

Sarah said, "I'm pretty sure your name is on several databases and you will be flagged. Be ready to take this one captive."

Su Li said, "Too late, look ahead of us." There were three unmarked cars coming toward them from the south, effectively blocking their escape route. There was no cover to either side for a quarter mile from the road.

Megan shook her head, "Dollars to doughnuts those cars are FBI. We're netted like fish in a barrel."

Sarah shook her head, "No we aren't. Laura, drive through or around them!"

Laura floored the Chevy and spun it in a circle. She shot past the Wyoming Sheriffs car as she headed back toward the main road they'd left. "We aren't going to be able to outrun them but we could confuse them. She suggested they pray for Yahveh's favor. They did pray as the Chevy tilted and swayed through the turns with the FBI cars quickly closing up from behind them.

As the first FBI car came close, Laura slammed on the brakes and made the FBI car swerve to the right to avoid a collision. Laura threw the Chevy into reverse and slammed into the left front fender of the government car causing it to cave in and blow the tire. The car swung sideward and came to a halt blocking the cars behind it because of the ditches on either side.

Laura floored the accelerator on the Chevy and raced away from the stalled cars. Sarah said, "You know they've got units coming at us from the roadblock, don't you?"

Laura grinned, "Yes, but we're going to disappear."

As they went through two s-curves Laura slowed down and then turned to the right and pulled up into the driveway of an empty house that had a "for sale" sign in the front yard. Sarah understood what Laura was doing and opened her door and jumped out. She ran to the garage door and found it locked. She took out two lock pick tools and had the lock undone in less than ten seconds. She opened the two-car garage door and Laura pulled the Chevy into the garage. Sarah shut the door. Everyone got out of the car and followed Sarah into the house proper.

Su Li asked, "What's the plan?

CHAPTER FORTY-SEVEN

Sarah sat down on the floor. "Not much, we will try to negotiate with the FBI who will have a squad of SWAT officers and their quasi-military anti-crime team as well as several snipers. Possibly, they'll have one or more armored vehicles. We can't run and we can't hide."

Christi asked, "Why can't we run?"

Su Li pointed up toward the ceiling. "They've got several small drones above us. That's why Laura pulled in here. This way, the FBI doesn't know what we have or what we're doing. But, it's just a stop gap. Eventually we will be apprehended."

They were there about fifteen minutes when they heard a bull-horn from the front of the house. *"This is the FBI. This house is surrounded by armed personnel. Put down any weapons you have and exit the house with your hands up or we will have to enter forcibly."*

Sarah just shook her head. "Do as the megaphone says. We don't have any options." She took out her pistol and unloaded it and put it on the floor.

Laura had been praying and suddenly said, "Wait a minute. Be quiet!" Sarah quickly reloaded her pistol.

The other three people stared at Laura. She smiled and reached down into her shirt and pulled out two ear buds on cords. She placed them into her ears. She spoke, "Yes, I hear you sweetheart. You have come just in time. Yes, Yes, Okay. Team two out."

She looked up and smiled. "The Cavalry is here!" Hide your weapons under your clothes."

Everyone stood up and waited. Sarah rolled her eyes realizing she had overlooked something important and found her own ear buds and put them in her ears.

Outside the small house in Southern Wyoming the lead agent for the FBI was losing his patience and was about to order the troops to go in and get these women.

Russ Holly was a senior agent and knew how to control every situation he was in charge of. He had direct orders from the Director of the FBI to capture these terroristic agents of the Crossfire Team. Nothing was going to stop him from carrying out his orders.

Suddenly he heard a crash behind him and he spun around to see a fireball and cloud of smoke rising from the ground. One of his support team said, "That was our number 1 observation and attack drone."

Russ was mad now. He was about to order the raid and he lost his best drone. He... There was another crash followed by four more, all in close proximity to their position. His tech threw up his hands. "There go all the rest of our drones!"

Russ was knocked over by an even bigger blast. He struggled back to his feet and stared at the huge fireball not five hundred feet from his location. "What was that?"

"That Sir was the only Predator drone we had. It had four, two-million-dollar Hellfire missiles on it too." The Tech Agent shut down all his gear since there was nothing to control.

Russ grabbed his cell phone only to find it didn't work. "What in blazes is going on here?"

A quiet but powerful sound, sort of a "whoosh" sounded and an ultra-futuristic aircraft settled to the ground fifty feet away from the lead agent. A side door opened and two men in full body armor and helmets exited the aircraft and walked up to the FBI agent.

Russ Holly looked at the dark sun visor and demanded, "Who are you and by what authority are you interfering with this investigation?"

Mark Connelly slid up the dark visor and looked calmly at the man. "My name is Mark Connelly of the Crossfire Team. I am advising you to break off your criminal assault on the women in this house immediately or suffer the consequences."

Russ sputtered and said, "You are the illegal terroristic party here. I am operating under the direct orders of the head of the FBI and the President of these United States. I demand you surrender immediately."

Mark shook his head. "The rule of Marco Marino is demonic and as criminal as you can get. Your One-World-Government was forced onto honest American citizens by a corrupt government that ceded your sovereignty, illegally, to the Anti-Christ in direct violation of the Constitution of these United States. As an agent of a corrupt government you are also in criminal violation of the commandments of God almighty. We are going to take our personnel and leave. I advise you again not to try to interfere. If you do, we will defend ourselves. In case you are stupid enough to think you can win a battle with us, remember your drones."

Mark used his battle-COMM and told David Zahavy to complete his assignment. The door opened on the side of the plane again and David exited the plane with a luggage case and walked past the men and to the front door of the house. He knocked and the door opened and he entered. The door closed and five minutes later it opened and David and the five women walked out and toward the plane. As they walked by Russ, Laura said, "Sorry about the damage to your car. You can have the one in the garage in compensation."

Russ had turned a bright shade of reddish pink and was so mad he could have spit nails. "No! I will not allow it!" He pulled his service pistol and aimed it at Mark. He shouted, "These people are not to leave here. I command them to stop. If they don't stop then I order every man under my command to use every weapon at their disposal to make them obey!"

Mark looked at the irate man. He walked closer to him. "Are you so stupid that you would order all of your men to die to satisfy your ego? You are an idiot."

Pushed past his limit, the agent lost control and fired four rounds directly into Mark's chest.

Mark reached out and took the gun away from the agent and threw it into the shrubbery by the side of the road. He shook his head and repeated his last word. "Idiot".

Seeing their lead agent in trouble, several of the other military tactical agents fired their rifles at Mark. Mark looked back at several of the firing agents and just shook his head. He walked back to the plane with Jack beside him. Rounds kept slamming into both men and the aircraft without effect.

After they boarded the Myth the door closed and the aircraft lifted straight up. One of the FBI agents fired an anti-tank missile at the aircraft and scored a direct hit which resulted in, nothing.

The Myth rose straight up at increasing speed until it arched over and headed toward Europe at Mach 6.

Sarah reached down and turned off her Force Generator and then hugged Mark. "Thanks for coming to rescue us." Mark hugged her back and then addressed the other four women. "I'm glad you were able to stay out of their hands until we got there. I was worried about having to pry you out of their grip if they had control of you. This was much better."

An urgent alarm and a voice announcement sounded. "There is an anti-missile, missile approaching on a collision course. Brace for impact in six seconds."

With an urgent tone Christi said, "What do we do?"

Laura smiled, "Watch and see the Hand of God defend us."

The missile struck with a great amount of smoke and flame and then quickly disappeared as the plane's greater speed left it behind.

Mark was praying his thanks to the Father when he got a word. He said, "Amein" and thought about the word he had received for a minute. Then he called Ethan in the COMM/SEC group. "Ethan, is the Senate of the United States meeting today?"

Ethan came back with, "Hold on for a minute."

He came back in less than a minute. "Yes, the majority of the Senate is meeting about an urgent bill right now. Why?"

Mark said, "I think we need to give them a good will visit."

CHAPTER FORTY-EIGHT

Jack looked at Mark, "Are you sure that's a good idea?"

Mark smiled, "It's not my idea." He pointed upward. "It's more of an order."

Jack sighed, "Then we go to Washington. How many of us are going into the Senate chambers?"

"All of us, that's what the Father of the Universe, wants and that's what He will get."

Jack called the R&D group at the Sea Base and gave them a change of flight schedules. They checked everything and approved the new arrangements.

The Myth immediately changed directions and headed back toward the East Coast of the U.S.

Jack got up from his seat and went to the Force Generator bolted to the air frame and switched it to the "Special" setting. He then told the other people, especially Christi, about the changes. "When you move the switch from "Normal" to "Special" you essentially become invisible. Nothing else changes as far as protection the field gives you. Christi, I will have Laura check you until you feel comfortable using the Force Generator, okay?"

Christi nodded, "Thanks, I didn't know these things existed until an hour ago."

Jack nodded back, "They are God's gift of protection for us in situations He feels needs equalization to allow us to do His will. Normally, He doesn't allow us to use them because then we would be invincible and that isn't balance either."

The myth landed in an open grassy area near the U.S. Capital building and the nine members of the Crossfire Team exited the invisible aircraft and walked through the Rotunda and into the Senate chamber. The men and women sitting at the old style desks were involved in a major vote and almost all of the Senators were there.

Being invisible the Team didn't cause any problems as they walked between people and up to the front of the chamber. On Mark's command they all switched their Force

Generators to "Normal" and suddenly became visible. That did cause a disturbance.

Jack held up his right hand and asked, "Will everyone please relax and settle down. We are not here to cause any problems. We just need to ask a question of this August body." Jack had a command voice and could be heard clearly by most of the Senators.

When the members quieted down, Jack addressed them. "Senators, I am Jack Malone of the Crossfire Team. Most of you should remember us. We defended the people and this country from many attempts to destroy the country. I realize it will be hard for you to put politics aside but I urge you to do that and listen to our message. We serve the Lord of the Universe who most of you know as God and His Son Jesus. He is the one that wants you to listen to God's message."

There was a loud gasp from many of the Senators as the angels Rose and Caleb appeared above the Speaker's podium. Everyone heard Caleb's voice clearly. "Senators of the United States Congress. Yahveh God has a word for you. *"My children, you are in the end times of the Gentiles on this earth. The enemy of all mankind, Satan, is vying for every heart and spirit among humanity. He is the power behind the Anti-Christ, Marco Marino. Beware, there is a judgment coming and I will bring that judgment on all humanity. This team of people I have anointed to do battle against the forces of evil are not your enemies. The One-World-Government labels them as terrorists but that is not true. They represent Me and as such are protected by Me. They do not want to hurt any Americans especially those that truly believe in truth and justice. But, I am not a man and I have given your people and your country as much leeway as I can."*

Four Senate Guards rushed into the chamber and Caleb made a gesture with his left hand. All four men froze in position. Caleb looked at the assembly. "God's Word is true, do not forget it." Both angels disappeared.

The four guards were suddenly mobile again and they rushed forward to arrest the Team. Two of the older Senators stood up and stepped into the guard's path, stopping them. The Senior Senator from Montana said,

"Leave these people alone. I am authorizing their presence. If we need you, we will call you. Now, leave us alone."

The guards were confused but the Senators made it clear they needed to leave, so they left.

After the guards were gone one Senator stood up and said, "I am on the Armed Services Committee and I am very aware of the tremendous services and victories your team has accomplished for our country. I applaud you. Be assured I will do all I can to champion your team."

Jack said, "Thank you Senator. I assure everyone here that we want only the best for the honest people of the United States. It will not be easy to do what God just told you because of the corruption of many in the Government. But please, I beg you; do not come under a curse from God. Thank you all for listening to us today in such abrupt manner. Have a blessed day. The Team walked out of the chamber and turned on the "Special" operation of the Force Generators and disappeared.

They made it back to the Myth and lifted off without any detection or attack. Soon, they were on their way back to the Sea Base.

Laura came up to Jack and Mark and asked, "What was that all about? God didn't really need us there. The angels could have appeared and God could have spoken to the Senators without our presence. Do you have any idea?"

Jack was about to agree with her when Mark smiled and said, "The reason he wanted us there was to personalize the message. It's too easy to explain away angels and announcements from God. We were God's example to the Senators. Sort of like the toy you took to school on show and tell day."

Laura thought about that, "Oh, joy."

CHAPTER FORTY-NINE

Christi was impressed by the location of the Sea Base and after a tour was even more impressed. She was assigned an apartment and that put her into impression overload. She decided she needed a good night's rest before she got down to why she came.

The next morning, after breakfast, she asked if she could talk with Jack and Laura. They agreed and took Christi back to their apartment and got comfortable in their living room. Laura smiled at the younger woman and asked, "Okay, what is on your mind?"

Christi smiled back. "I am somewhat confused and I'm hoping you guys can clarify things for me."

Jack and Laura sat there patiently.

Christi sighed, "Okay, four weeks ago I had a dream in which the angel Rose told me I had been assigned a "mission" by the Father. She didn't explain what that mission was or how I was to do it. Then two weeks later came the dream where I was shown how to use a sword and all the tactics necessary to win sword battles. I realized later that I was probably in the heavenly realm for some time, because the increase in my muscle size and tone, especially in my arms and shoulders couldn't have happened overnight in a dream. Then, two nights ago I was threatened by a demon. I heard a voice telling me to pray continuously and the armor and sword appeared. I can tell you that I was completely at a loss as to what to do with them until this rush of tactics and moves flooded my mind along with how to use them. I was able to defeat the demon and that led me to call you, Jack, and to come here. Well, here I am. What do we do?"

Laura laughed, "It's simple. Christi, we pray.

She settled into the prayer with much greater ease than she thought that she would. She glanced around the apartment quickly to settle her mind as to her physical location. Her step-brother, Jack Malone, and his wife, Laura Malone were kneeling on the floor as they begin to pray.

Christi felt like a novice next to these two spiritual warriors whose combat frequently shifted over to the physical. Still, she felt camaraderie with both of them and everyone else she had met who belonged to the Crossfire Team. She knew she was kneeling in a plush apartment with a view of the sea waves rolling into the rocks under the apartment as she could see through the open French doors. The rhythmic sounds of the waves and the exotic smell of the Mediterranean Sea brought a peace to her soul. The fact that they were almost a mile below the surface of the sea wasn't obvious. She was here because an angel called Rose had told her to come here to find out what the God of the Universe wanted her to do. She was here to define her "mission".

She closed her eyes and prayed passionately from her heart to a God that she knew was listening to them. As they praised Yahveh she fell deeper into the prayer and felt something like a pressure or a tension in the air.

Sensing something different she opened her eyes to an exceptional sight. An angel she had seen before floated two feet over the floor. He was a big angel and had fiery eyes and a robe of such whiteness it glared.

Jack opened his eyes. "Greetings and blessings Caleb, mighty warrior. Are you here to answer our prayer?"

Caleb's voice was a deep bass the vibrated in the air. Christi was awed by his presence.

Caleb floated over near Christi. "Greetings Christi Steele, I am pleased to greet you in the name of the Most High." That vibration was inside of her now. She smiled at the angel. "I am pleased to meet you also, Caleb. Are you here to tell me what my importance to the Crossfire Team is? And what mission God has for me?"

Caleb looked at her and through her for several seconds. "I am here to bring you a word from the Most High." "Christi, my child, I love you with a burning love that will sustain you in the times to come. You have a unique ability of which you are not aware of as yet. But, that talent is critical to the survival of the Crossfire Team. I brought you here to fulfill your destiny that I assigned to you before you were born. Do not fear or concern yourself as to your future. You will understand everything at the proper time. See, when it comes to pass you will remember *that I have told you so. Grow into the warrior I made you to be. Learn from the Team and be strong. Your light will shine like a mighty sun that will cause the enemy to flee from you. I will be with you and I will not forsake you."*

Caleb placed his hand on her head and a white force seemed to flood her whole being. "Stay true to the Most High's commands and walk in righteousness. We will be with you also."

Caleb faded out of view. Christi closed her eyes and prayed her thanks and love to Yahveh. She got to her feet and grinned at Jack and Laura. "Okay, I still don't know what my mission is but apparently it is to train with you guys until my "special unique talent is revealed". She thought for a second. "Just what talent could I have that could even be anywhere near what you guys have?"

Laura smiled back at her. "We are all simply servants of the Most High. Each one of us has talents that added together make the Team what it is, a tool for God to use to help others. Welcome to the Team, Christi. Why don't we figure out the normal daily things for you to live with us?" Laura looked introspective for a few seconds and then came over and took Christi's hands in hers. "I'm sorry, we are so used to doing what the Father tells us to do, that I never thought to ask you if this is something that you want to do?"

Christi squeezed Laura's hands and let her go. She sat down on one of the sofas and sighed. Looking up at her relative, she smiled. "I came to realize, on our little chase around Wyoming, that I missed being with you, and Sarah, and the excitement, danger, miracles, and everything else. After the battle with the demon, the armor and sword, and then everything since then that this is my destiny. It doesn't ring true in my spirit that I am going to be a wife and mother. Lately there is something, not quite right with my life. The last two days have shown me what I was missing. I believe it is my destiny to serve God However He wants me to. After hearing from Caleb I think my destiny is here with you, and Jack, and Sarah. I hope you don't think I am butting in on the Team."

Jack laughed out loud. "It isn't our Team, it belongs to Yahveh and when He told you to learn, train, become one of us it was settled. It's not our call but, I would have voted for you to join us without that. When you told me that Yahveh trained and gave you the armor and sword and you already battled a demon, I knew you would be a Team Mate. Welcome aboard."

Laura pulled her up from the sofa and hugged her, "That goes for me also."

Christi said, "I am going to be the best me I can be for the Team. I have to be, Caleb told me I would be."

Jack stood up and hugged Christi. "Come on; let us introduce you to the rest of your new team mates." They left the apartment and headed for the War Room.

Christi didn't feel that special but the Lord of the Universe said that she was, therefore it must be true. Still she felt very humble to have this opportunity.

As they walked into the War Room she recognized four of the people there. She saw Sarah, Mark, Megan, and Su Li. Walking over to them she hugged them all. They all hugged her back. Jack called her over to a seat next to Megan.

Jack had her sit down and explained the operation of the console and showed her the lists of numbers and things she could do. It was impressive, but it was similar enough to a panel she used to use at one of her previous jobs that it didn't look like too big of a challenge.

One by one the other core team members came in to use the War Room or dropped in to see someone that was there. They all were introduced to Christi and welcomed her. Su Li warned her about the amorous characters such as Elon and Ethan. "They are cute and it is flattering but I would keep my distance until you get your bearings. They could be a problem since you are single and very attractive."

Christi actually blushed, "Thank you for the warning and the compliment. I'll take your advice."

After the new people coming to the War Room slacked off, Sarah came over to Christi and invited her to the breakfast nook/snack bar for a coffee.

After they were seated Sarah asked, "Are you getting a little dizzy with all the new faces?"

Christi smiled, "A little, but I'll keep working until I know who's who."

Sarah nodded, "That's the spirit. To help you figure out who is who and what they do, there is a file on your computer in your apartment called WHO.org. That will give you a chance to put a face to a name."

CHAPTER FIFTY

Sarah lead Christi over to the SOG Barracks and told her to find her again when she got back. Then she left.

Christi walked up to the Barracks Orderly Station and inquired about her two brothers who were stationed there.

Reve Colton showed Christi how to look up the locations for both soldiers. Then she looked at Christi, "You are their sister, right?"

Christi nodded, "Yep, that's my lot in life. Did you grow up with older brothers?"

Reve smiled, "Just one bigger brother. He was my protector which was great until I wanted to start dating. Then he felt he needed to keep me away from all boys."

Christi shook her head. "You should have heard the warnings I got about dating Marines. I did it anyway because it was something denied me. They were right."

Thanking Reve, Christi headed down to the exercise facility in search of Craig and Kevin Steele. She slipped into the busy room and took a seat near the door. It didn't take her long to spot Craig. He had a particular way of standing when he wasn't working out. But, she couldn't find Kevin.

Craig finished his routine and was heading out of the training room to take a shower when he heard a sweet voice from his past. "Are you going to even say hello?"

He stopped and stared at his little sister. "Don't you know you shouldn't hang around this kind of crowd?"

He stopped her from hugging him. "I'm covered in sweat and as Mom would say, "I'm ripe." Craig smiled at her. "You are a sight for sore eyes. How are you? What are you doing here?"

Christi laughed, "I couldn't let you two clowns have all the fun. Yahveh told me to come down here and make sure you're doing the right things. Where is Kevin?"

Craig looked around, "There he is working the wrestling mat like normal. He is good at it but I don't want to get that close to a demon or a bad guy. I'd just rather shoot them or carve them up with my sword. Look, I'm going to clean up, hang around and we can talk then."

Christi nodded, "Okay, big brother." After Craig left she watched Kevin wrestle for a while. Then Craig came back and they left the exercise room and went to the SOG Canteen for a drink and a snack.

Suitably supplied with a power drink and some peanuts they found a table they could sit at and talk. Craig eyed his little sister, "How come you don't have an escort? Normally, visitors have to have an escort to get in this section."

Christi decided it was time to fill him in on her change in life. "Craig, I'm not a visitor. I'm a part of the Crossfire Team now."

Craig looked at her and believed she was pulling his leg. He was about to laugh when something in her attitude and seriousness made him reconsider. "Oh, really, what do you do for the team?"

Christi looked down and then back up into his eyes. "I am a part of the Core Team." Seeing the disbelief in his eyes she smiled. "Three days ago I was given golden armor and fought a demon and killed it. That was back in Denver. Since then I've been chased by the FBI, cornered along with Laura, Sarah, Su Li, and Megan Cole in a house by dozens of troops. I've gotten to wear a Force Generator and stand in the Senate Chamber in the U.S. Capital and fly in the Myth. I've met the angel Caleb and listened to Yahveh's words telling me that I will be a crucial part of the Team and it was His arrangement for me to be here. That's how I got a position here. What I am going to do hasn't been explained as yet. I apparently have some special anointing or talent that will show up when it is needed. So, how about that, coworker?"

Craig wanted to deny her but his spirit confirmed what she had said as the truth. "Wow! In three days? I guess I'm going to have to keep an eye on you to keep you safe. Or maybe you'll have to keep me safe. I am amazed, but, welcome aboard, sister."

They reminisced for a while and then Craig had an assignment he had to go to. He hugged Christi and told her he loved her and wanted updates, frequent updates.

Christi smiled and told him she'd do the best she could to keep him in the loop.

She went back to Reve only to find out that Kevin was on assignment with the Tel Aviv Police until 9:00 P.M. that night.

She made her way back to the living room and went upstairs to freshen up when she ran into her mother.

There was some shock on both sides. "Mom! What are you doing here?"

Donna Malone said, "I was going to say the same thing. Why are you here? I'm really glad to see you, I've missed you."

Christi said, "I thought you went in the Rapture. What happened?"

Her mother explained their escape to Israel and what they were doing here. "Steve is here along with Larry and Gavina. They are going to be surprised and happy to see you. We thought you'd gone in the Rapture also.

Christi repeated what she had told Craig. Donna was amazed, concerned and happy that her daughter would be so close.

Christi said, "We'll have to get together and talk. I've got to clean up and find Sarah; she wants to start my training I think."

They hugged and promised to see each other soon.

CHAPTER FIFTY-ONE

Christi found Sarah talking with Laura in the War Room. She waited until Sarah was free and then approached her. "Well, I found one, missed one, and found one I didn't know was here."

Sarah cocked her head to the left. "Who was here you didn't know about?"

Christi told Sarah about her mom. "I was out of Denver when the Rapture happened. I was in Southern California for my job at the time. I was disappointed when I realized that I didn't go in the Rapture but not terribly. I believe that Yahveh gave me a strange peace about that because of what is happening right now. I tried to reach my mom but the phones were down and I was sure she went in the Rapture anyway. By the time I returned to Denver she had moved with my step-father because of the hatred that the Anti-Christ created to blame the Christians for the Rapture causing all the damage and social unrest."

Christi took a drink of her coffee.

"It was a shock but I had to carry on and it wasn't really a deep concern. It was probably more of the same peace. I didn't realize how much I missed her until I saw her here."

Sarah could agree but her mother had passed away years ago and it was a moot argument for her. She began to tell the newest member of the Team about many things. Christi listened and took notes and learned a great deal.

Christi asked about the Force Generators because she was fascinated by the devices. Sarah filled her in on the development and uses of the devices and the fact that the Father in Heaven would only let them use the Generators to correct imbalances between the Crossfire Team and whoever they were in combat with at the time. The majority of the time they didn't have the Generators to protect them. The fact that all hell was concentrated on the Team was sufficient for the Team to use the Generators all the time.

Then Sarah explained about the three new aspects of the devices, one of which Christi had already used. She had used the aspect of becoming basically invisible. Also, she had watched Jack use the ability to make the Myth invisible. Christi asked about the other two aspects. Sarah smiled, "A very useful is the ability of the field to prevent being held in one position. You can use one of two methods of escape. Both are actually spiritually powered in performance. If you become stuck in a position and want to extradite yourself, you simply have to "will" your Force Generator to move in a certain direction."

"Yahveh's Holy Spirit uses the elemental forces of the universe to power the move. For example, if you are buried in sand you can will yourself to move sideward or upward and the Force Generator field will move that way as far as you want because God will take you there. The same method will work if you're buried under ten tons of rocks or in a thick steel box."

Christi was in awe. "That is great! What is the other method of escape?"

Sarah grinned; this one was right up her alley. "Number two is far more destructive. If your shield is on and you are prevented from moving in a direction by say, a wall, you can focus your mind, rather than your will, and "see" the obstacle in front of you removed. It has been tried to make sure it works. There is a very solid building missing because of that one effort. It is an extremely dangerous power. Be careful of collateral damage if you ever employ it."

As part of her training, Sarah took Christi to the surface and out to some deserted factory buildings that provided a covered area to use the Force Generator without observation. Christi practiced using both the "moves" and the "destroys" features on a very small scale. The "destroys" feature turned another one of the deserted buildings, the asphalt parking area and everything inside the building to fragments.

Christi turned off the Generator and stood there in shock over the destruction she had caused with a very small movement. Sarah solemnly nodded her head. "You should have seen the destruction we caused simply by falling on two buildings in Zyngola, Africa about a year ago."

Christi's eyebrow lifted, "Falling on two buildings?"

Sarah nodded again. "Yes, from 40,000 feet without a parachute. We were falling missiles inside of the Force Generators. We obliterated a four story office building which was also the command center for the base. There was nothing and no one left standing."

Christi nodded her head. "Laura got me her after-action report on that action. I was in awe of her combat with the strong man, too."

Sarah took her back to the Undersea Base and set up an overall training regimen for Christi. She handed it to Christi and indicated the times and dates. "You will learn combat arms and combat from my husband, Mark. You will study advanced sword techniques from Jack. I've got you scheduled for Martial Arts instruction from Su Li and sometimes Jack. You'll learn communications and security systems from Charlie Wu and his wife Linda. I did that because I don't want you to have to spend one-on-one time with Ethan Reaper. Not yet. Nice guy but still young, single, and impulsive, a dangerous combination around a pretty girl. I've also got you scheduled for classes in spirituality and especially, spiritual warfare with Laura. Lastly, both Linda Wu and I will teach you spy craft. I was trained by the Mossad and Linda was a state agent for the Chinese Internal Security forces."

Sarah sat back in her chair. "Don't worry about all this training. You need it and you look like a quick learner. As you reach the teacher's goals for you, you will only need refresher classes.

Outside the human dimension, Caleb asked Rose, "Do you think she will be up to the task the Most High has assigned her?"

Rose smiled, "I do, I really do."

The Crossfire Team will return in:
"ALBATROSS CROSSFIRE"

If this story has awakened you or moved you to seek the love of Christ and His power for your life, whether you've never accepted Jesus as your savior or you've fallen away, repeat the following prayer and begin a most wonderful journey into eternal life with Him today.

Father God in heaven, As You said in Your Holy Word, (Romans 10:9) that if we confess the Lord Jesus as our God and believe in our hearts that by His Holy Spirit Yahveh God raised Jesus from the dead, we shall be saved.

(The prayer on the next page is a sample prayer when asking Jesus into your heart as your Savior. You can also pray this in your own words.)

Salvation Prayer

Dear God in heaven, I come to you in the name of Jesus. I confess to You that I am a sinner, and I am sorry for my sins and the life that I have lived; I need your forgiveness. I believe that your only begotten Son Jesus Christ shed His precious blood on the cross at Calvary and died for my sins, and I am now willing to turn from my sin.

Right now I confess Jesus as the Lord of my life and my soul. With all my heart, I truly believe that your Holy Spirit raised Jesus from the dead. Today I accept Jesus Christ as my personal Savior and according to Your Word, right now I am saved.

I thank you Jesus, for your unlimited grace which has saved me from my sins. I thank you Jesus that your grace that never leads to license, but rather it always leads to repentance. Therefore Lord Jesus, transform my life so that I may bring glory and honor to you alone and not to myself.

I thank you Lord Jesus, for dying for me at Calvary and giving me eternal life.

Amen.

If you just said this prayer and you meant it with all your heart, believe that you are now saved and have been born again.

You may ask, "Now that I am saved, what do I do next?" First of all you need to get into a spirit-filled, bible-based church that teaches the Scriptures, and you need to study God's Word.

Once you have found a church home, you will want to become water-baptized by immersion. By accepting Christ you are baptized in the spirit, but it is through water-baptism that you publically announce your obedience to the Lord Jesus. Water baptism is a symbol of your salvation from the dead. You were dead but now you live, for Jesus Christ has redeemed you for a price! The price was His atoning death on the cross. May God Bless You as you learn to walk in His light!

www.ingramcontent.com/pod-product-compliance
Lightning Source LLC
Chambersburg PA
CBHW060934180626
46817CB00004B/1541